Sir John Skelton

**Charles I**

Sir John Skelton

**Charles I**

ISBN/EAN: 9783742864963

Manufactured in Europe, USA, Canada, Australia, Japa

Cover: Foto ©Andreas Hilbeck / pixelio.de

Manufactured and distributed by brebook publishing software
(www.brebook.com)

Sir John Skelton

# Charles I

# CHARLES I.

CHARLES I

# CHARLES I.

BY

SIR JOHN SKELTON, K.C.B.

GOUPIL & CO.,
FINE ART PUBLISHERS.
JEAN BOUSSOD, MANZI, JOYANT & CO.,
SUCCESSORS,
FINE ART PUBLISHERS TO HER MAJESTY.

LONDON:
25, BEDFORD STREET, STRAND.

PARIS:
24, BOULEVARD DES CAPUCINES.

EDINBURGH:
W. BROWN, 26, PRINCES STREET.

1898.

# PUBLISHERS NOTE.

It is with the greatest regret the Publishers have to state that the author of *Charles I.* died last year. Sir John Skelton, who was knighted at the time of the Diamond Jubilee, had been in weak health, but he worked diligently at the volume up to the day of his death, on 19th July, 1897. He had written the whole of the text and revised it up to the middle of the last chapter, and it has not been found necessary, after the most competent examination, to alter the author's work in any particular. Every care has been taken to insure accuracy, and it is hoped that textual errors have been entirely avoided. The Publishers desire to thank the owners of the originals of the beautiful illustrations of the volume. The majority are from works in the Royal Collections, Her Majesty the Queen having very graciously given instructions to permit the Publishers to select what they considered best for this purpose. This selection has been left to the care of Mr. D. C. Thomson, Editor of the *Art Journal*, who has also arranged the other plates. The Publishers thank the authorities of the Louvre, His Grace the Duke of Westminster, His Grace the Duke of Buccleuch, the Earl of Radnor, the Earl of Buckinghamshire, and the Earl of Rosebery, for the use of unique and famous works of art. To the Committee of the House of Lords for permission to reproduce the Death Warrant, the Society of Antiquaries, and the authorities of the British Museum and South Kensington Museum, for assistance of various kinds, they also tender their cordial thanks.

HER MAJESTY THE QUEEN

ACCEPTED

THE DEDICATION OF THIS VOLUME

FROM THE AUTHOR.

# PRELUDE.

The place of Charles I. in English constitutional history is a matter of supreme interest on which, however, no authoritative verdict can be pronounced until his relation to those who went before him, and to those who came after him, has been duly examined, and at least provisionally settled. We cannot judge him fairly unless we know something of the Tudors; something of the Scottish family who were to wear the English Crown; something of Cromwell and the Commonwealth: something, too, of the later Stuarts. Not otherwise, in my humble judgment, can the due historical perspective be maintained. Forced as I am to work under stringent limitations, there is risk, I can see, of overcrowding the canvas. But now that the evidence has been led and the facts ascertained (and it is impossible to speak too highly of the unwearied industry which has made our national records easily accessible), the narrative will admit of reasonable compression; and, with Vandyke to help us, the portraits may be in miniature. On one or two of the most striking episodes, it will be convenient and interesting to enlarge; but the reader who desires to make close acquaintance with the varied incidents and the motley actors in a prolonged constitutional struggle, must turn to the monumental work of Samuel Rawson Gardiner.

The whole subject is eminently controversial; and, after all that has been written, one cannot but feel that the debate has not been concluded. The Stuart Kings of England are at the bar. Guilty or not guilty? They have been bitterly assailed; they have been eagerly defended. Can any middle way be found? An intemperate partisanship defeats itself. I am not prepared to maintain that they governed with eminent wisdom, or that theirs was a policy which high political sagacity would have dictated or approved. But, on the other hand, the strain of the political situation was great, and they laboured, as we shall see, under special disabilities. Taking all the circumstances into account, is it fair to allege (for this is the specific charge on which they are being tried) that they subverted, or tried to subvert, the Constitution?

The line I propose to follow may be briefly indicated. I propose to inquire, in the first place, what, under the Tudors, was the recognised relation between the Parliament, the People, and the Sovereign? I do not go further back, because it appears to me that, so far as Charles, so far as the Stuart Kings, may be held to be culpable, the *practice* between the accession of Henry VII. in 1485, and the death of Elizabeth in 1603, is, if not the sole, the most material, factor. The precedents of a hundred and twenty years cannot be lightly displaced. The Tudors were autocratic no doubt; but it is not denied that, *upon the whole*, the ancient constitutional maxims, so far as applicable, were fairly observed by them. "So far as applicable;" for the conditions had changed. It was of course in the province of ecclesiastical polity that the change was most marked. The Church of the Tudors was not the Church of the Plantagenets; the King of England had taken the place of the Bishop of Rome; the Papal supremacy had been exchanged for the Royal. No precedents drawn from ecclesiastical law or usage prior to the Reformation could, when Elizabeth died, be regarded as binding. If it was assumed by the Stuarts when they came to England that the constitutional compact which they were bound to observe had taken definitive form during the sixteenth century, they may have erred, but the error was not unnatural.

The annals of the Scottish line of Kings, up to the day when James VI. left his ancient capital, must then be rapidly reviewed. The fact that the Stuarts were unfamiliar with the people that they came to govern no doubt explains much. The experience they had gained in Scotland could be of little service to them in the South,—was indeed but indifferent preparation for the novel part they were called on to play. Their racial feuds with Scottish nobles, their acrid controversies with Scottish ecclesiastics, had not involved any large or intricate questions of constitutional law. A rude society, still profoundly feudal, was used to plainer methods. Maitland of Lethington was, as Elizabeth said, "the flower of the wits of Scotland;" but Maitland was in truth an altogether exceptional figure; on the one hand, the hardy moss-trooper, on the other, the austere fanatic, were the exponents of law and gospel across the Tweed. Then there was a strain not exactly of madness, but of moodiness, in the Stuart temperament. The evil Fate that attended the House had left tragic reminiscences. The sense of persistent ill-luck haunted them to the end. Not mad exactly; but the alternate fits of gaiety and gloom, of obstinacy and languor (from which no Stuart was free) are symptomatic of mental disturbance.

The Union of the Crowns could not thus be regarded as an unmixed blessing either for the rulers or the ruled. The initial difficulties under the most favourable conditions must have been considerable; but the problems which the Stuart Kings of England were asked to solve were, it must be admitted, well-nigh insoluble. They would have baffled Henry VIII. himself; were, on her death-bed, baffling Elizabeth. Henry and Elizabeth were mainly responsible indeed for the special forms which the vast forces which had been set in motion by Humanist and Reformer had taken in England. Even at the time there were men who foresaw that the Tudor policy would one day lead to war. There was, it may be, a happy moment when conciliation might have disarmed hostility. But it was allowed to pass, and the gulf had widened,—had widened into an impassable chasm.

It may be asserted with absolute confidence that, while the Seventeenth Century was yet in its teens, no cunning device, no sobriety of judgment, no lucidity of intelligence, could have averted the constitutional struggle that was at hand. Its development into civil strife was in the circumstances inevitable. Try as they might, both sides were helpless; they were driven on, as in Homeric battle, by the Gods, or, as we say now, by an imperious necessity. It was one of those cases in which, from an apparently trivial misunderstanding at the outset, a feud arises which must be fought out to the bitter end, and which cannot be stayed until one or other of the combatants is exhausted. In such conflicts it is often difficult to determine which side deserves to win. Our new schools of political thought are somewhat intolerant; and though a minority may still believe that "the right of private judgment" is valuable to those only who are capable of using it with wisdom, and that the weight of too much liberty is apt to become oppressive, yet the majority, in their devotion to democratic rule, have turned "freedom" into a fetish. The doctrine of passive obedience was held at the time to have scriptural warrant; the same authority was invoked by the men who resisted the Lord's Anointed even unto death. Into these high regions of speculation the lay historian may prudently decline to venture; the abstract right of subjects to rebel, of rulers to repress rebellion, being one of those conundrums which may be discussed till Domesday,—the answer varying according to time and locality and individual temperament. During one age the right divine of the wise to counsel the ignorant and control the foolish, in other words, the commanding authority of ripe experience, will be freely acknowledged; whereas in an age of intellectual restiveness and restlessness, of pride in nonconformity, of hunger for change, it is treated with disrespect or derision. But putting all these problems aside, the practical question that has to be resolved, when we come to deal with the prolonged quarrel between Charles and the Commons, is simply, Who was truly the aggressor? By whom was the *status quo ante bellum* disturbed? Are we to blame Charles and Strafford and Laud? or Pym and Vane and Cromwell?

The death of Charles, it is no paradox to say, was the cause of a temporary recoil in the advancing tide of Democracy. The flood-gates were closed again. The social, political, and religious forces which made for change were meantime checked. The Commonwealth meant the strong hand of the Army—the genius of Cromwell—nothing more. The English as a people did not accept it; on the contrary it was regarded by them with impatience and resentment; and the mad revel of the Restoration was the reply that they gave. The folly of the second Charles, and the fanaticism of the second James, turned the tide once more in the direction which, even under a Harley, a Walpole, or a North, it has ever since maintained. Democracy, it may be assumed, was bound to win sooner or later—as it has indeed won in the qualified form of a monarchy controlled by the Commons; but had the King's life been spared we might to-day have been citizens of the Republic founded by Oliver. The execution of Charles was not only an "inexpiable" crime,—it was the crowning blunder.

"SOVEREIGN OF THE SEAS."

From an old print by J. Payne.

# CHARLES THE FIRST.

## CHAPTER ONE.

### THE ENGLISH CONSTITUTION UNDER THE TUDORS.

When Henry Richmond on the field of Bosworth assumed the Crown, the Catholic Church was still powerful in England, and the New Learning had made comparatively little progress. The life, both civic and religious, was still ruled by a code which had been framed in the Middle Ages. The genius of the medieval architect had made our cities picturesque; and the ceremonies of medieval Catholicism, splendidly decorative, lent the colour that might be needed. What a spectacle to the rustic coming from outlying marsh or woodland—and in those days a third of the land at least was marsh and woodland—must a Cathedral city have presented. We may compare the august ritual of Rome unfavourably with a simpler service; but only the narrowest fanaticism can treat it with ridicule. In that communion there were then as now—let Puritanism say what it may—many pure and spiritually minded men, who were able to rise above the allurements of sense, and to behold, beyond the smoke of the incense and the gloom of the sanctuary, the vision of a righteous Judge. Nor was it in the Cathedral city alone that the Church wielded an unquestioned authority. With uncompromising energy it had penetrated into fen and forest. It shared the most absolute solitudes with the wild animals of the chase. Centuries had passed since Canute and his Knights, lying on their oars, had listened to the even-song of the Monks of Ely: and men who shrank from the rough issues of common life still practised, upon the Marsh of Romney or among the Lincoln Washes, the perilous virtues of the cloister.

Yet it was true that somehow or other, the whole of the spacious edifice had been undermined, and that it was tottering to its fall. Mitred ecclesiastics in the privacy of the chapter house might still discuss the policy of princes without any sense of impending doom. The faith once delivered to the Saints was still expounded in remote hamlet, or crowded city, by faithful servants of the Most High. But behind the fair show there was, it cannot be doubted, foul decay. The written record remains. Too often the monastic building has become a den of thieves; too often the nun, the bride of Heaven, is as shameless as the monk. Pilgrims swarming with vermin swarm along the highways, filthy mendicants recount their filthy adventures at this or the other shrine, pardoners dispose of their stale wares cheaply to gaping rustics. The popular satirist must not be taken too literally: and we are not bound to believe that the French-hood and *bon-grace* of the Virgin, the great toe of the Trinity, the jawbone of All-Saints, and the bees that stang Eve when she ate the apple, were hawked about; yet only a few years later, when the visitation of the monasteries was proceeding, Layton wrote to Cromwell from the Priory of Maiden Bradley;—"By my servant I sende yowe relyquis, fyrste, two flowres wrappede in white and blake sarcenet that one Christynmas evyn *hora ipsa qua Christus natus fuerat* will spring and burgen and bere blossoms, *quod expertum esse*, saith the prior off Maden Bradeley; ye shall also receve a bage of reliquis, wherein ye shall se straingeis thynges, as shall appere by the scripture, as Oure lades smoke, Parte of Godes supper *in cena domini*, *Pars petre super qua natus erat Jesus in Bethelem*, belyke ther is in Bethelem plentie of stones, and makith ther maingierres off stone. The scripture of evere thyng shall declare yowe all; and all thes of Maden Bradeley, wheras is an holy prior, and hath but six children, and but one dowghter mariede yet of the goodes of the monasterie, trystyng shortly to mary the reste..... I send yowe also oure lades gyrdell of Bruton, rede silke, wiche is a solemne reliquie sent to women travelyng, wiche shall not miscarie *in partu*." The scandal was open; it was noised abroad; it became the subject of common jest and satire. When lines like Heywood's lines penned, be it observed, by a devout Catholic,—

> "With small cost and without any paine,
> These *pardons* bring them to Heaven plaine;
> Give me but a penny or two pence,
> And as soon as the soul departeth hence,
> In half an hour, or three quarters at most,
> The soul is in Heaven with the Holy Ghost,—"

when lines like these could be listened to, not only without protest, but with keenest relish by a Catholic audience, the end could not be far off. The change indeed from one extreme to the other came with startling rapidity. Within a hundred years of Henry's death, one half of England was Puritan.

Whatever precautions might be taken, a vast spiritual confederacy, thoroughly organised, could not but be a menace to liberty. It was easier on the other hand to protect the life and property of the subject against an arbitrary exercise of the prerogative of the Crown; and on paper, it may be, ample guarantees had been given. The Great Charter itself was only one of a series of measures designed to preserve the freedom of the English Commonalty. Where the spirit of a free people is absent, legislation is well nigh worthless;—either by fraud or force, it can be evaded by an unscrupulous ruler. Against the tyranny of Prince and Priest, the Englishman was protected less by legislation, than by his own sturdy independence of character and the action of his municipal system. Excepting the greater nobles, who during the dynastic wars had been nearly exterminated, the gentry were mostly resident on their estates. Some of them occasionally proceeded to Westminster for the transaction of parliamentary business; but the hardship of being sent there was so great—although the burgesses at least had been paid for their attendance—that the Crown had frequently to compel the shires and burghs to elect representatives. Impassable roads infested by highwaymen, wretched hostels infested with vermin, made it a matter of labour and peril to reach the Metropolis from a distant county. Thus each district of the Kingdom continued to preserve within itself the elements of an independent and vigorous society. The gentry were the natural leaders of a pastoral people, with whom, on their many national and religious festivals, they familiarly mingled. To the classes engaged in commerce, the local guilds and the great trading societies supplied an obvious basis of co-operation and defence. A system which concentrates in the capital the whole machinery of Government is apt to weaken and enervate the national life; and though it is true that the bye-laws of the County-Courts, and of the burgh magistrates, were conceived in a peculiarly hostile and narrow spirit, yet it was fortunate for England that the discharge of civic duties and the exercise of local government had made the English layman, the yeoman as well as the gentleman, tenacious of his rights and jealous of his liberties.

There were two constitutional questions that came to the front in the prolonged and bitter quarrel between the Stuarts and their Parliaments. 1. What was the compact between the Houses and the Sovereign as to the revenues of the Crown,—the revenues by which the Royal State was to be maintained? 2. Had there been any illegal exercise of the royal prerogative (*a*) as regarded taxation, (*b*) as regarded the liberty of the subject, (*c*) as regarded religion? It is in the settlement of these questions that the practice of the Tudors is instructive. There is the further question of how far the Tudors themselves were responsible for the conditions, social, political ecclesiastical, which made the quarrel inevitable. The resistance to Charles in Parliament and in the country was conducted mainly by the Puritans. But for the harsh and oppressive laws of Elizabeth, there would have been, so far as we can judge, few, if any, Puritans. For the Puritan, therefore, Elizabeth must be held responsible. No doubt other forces than religion were at work. How far these contributed to make the crisis acute, we shall see hereafter. But it may be said generally that they were all due, more or less directly, to the spirit of unrest which the Reformation, the New Learning, the discovery of other worlds in the heaven above and on the earth beneath, had provoked. The temper of the time was Revolutionary, and Charles was its first victim. Between Revolution and the reaction from Revolution, excess on either side is probably inevitable. If democratic theories of Government had not been in the air, less would have been heard of the Divine Right of Kings.

On a casual survey one would have been inclined to conclude that, during the Tudor regime at any rate, the monarch was sufficiently absolute. Except on rare occasions, when popular indignation was keenly roused, any control exercised by the Parliament was nominal. There may have been in theory constitutional limitations; in practice it was Personal Rule. The very names of the parliamentary leaders have been forgotten; whereas the personality of Henry VIII. or of Elizabeth is stamped indelibly upon the national record. They had great ministers; Wolsey, Cromwell, Cecil; but none of these statesmen derived his force from Parliament, or owed his elevation to eminence in parliamentary counsel or debate. Yet the historians who have argued that the exercise of the Kingly authority was subject to restraints, sanctioned by ancient statute and immemorial usage, which even the most arbitrary and autocratic of the Tudors did not care to disregard, are not without warrant for their view.

Mr. Hallam has observed that at the accession of the Tudors the essential checks upon the royal authority were five in number: "1. The King could levy no sort of new tax upon his people, except by the grant of the Parliament consisting as well of bishops and mitred abbots or lords spiritual, and of hereditary peers or temporal lords, who sat and voted promiscuously in the same chamber, as of representatives from the freeholders of each county, and from the burgesses of many towns and less considerable places, forming the lower or commons house. 2. The previous assent and authority of the same assembly was necessary for every new law, whether of a general or temporary nature. 3. No man could be committed to prison but by a legal warrant specifying his offence, and by an usage nearly tantamount to constitutional right, he must be speedily brought to trial by means of regular sessions of gaol-delivery. 4. The fact of guilt or innocence on a criminal charge was determined in a public court, and in the county where the offence was alleged to have occurred, by a jury of twelve men, from whose unanimous verdict no appeal could be made. Civil rights, so far as they depended on questions of fact, were subject to the same decision. 5. The officers and servants of the Crown, violating the personal liberty or other right of the subject, might be sued in an action for damages to be assessed by a jury, or in some cases were liable to criminal process; nor could they plead any warrant or command in their justification, nor even the direct order of the King."

If indeed these checks existed (and no doubt they did on paper) it can hardly be denied, I think, except possibly by the legal pedant, that up to the close of Elizabeth's reign they had been habitually evaded. The Parliaments of the Tudors were in one sense "servile;" the great ecclesiastical reforms that were being carried through during years of peril and despondency required undivided counsel; and so long as the national credit was maintained, both peers and commons were content to acquiesce. The Crown had no doubt many creatures of its own in either House; arbitrary measures were taken to secure a loyal representation; but unless the people had been fairly satisfied that Monarch and Minister might be trusted to do their best for England, there would have been petitions and protests. One cannot help feeling that in such "servility" there was a touch of patriotism which later Parliaments might have imitated with advantage. Yet even these servile Parliaments were often dispensed with. Years would pass before their attendance was required at Westminster. Elizabeth was penurious by

CHARLES I.

*(With Ermine Robe.)*

From the painting by Sir Anthony Vandyke, in the Collection of Her Majesty the Queen, at Windsor Castle.

CHARLES I.

With Signing Rule

Vandyke, in the Col

at Windsor Castle.

nature; and though Henry VIII. was recklessly profuse, the savings of his father and the spoils of the monastries were immense. It is true that most of the Church lands went to greedy nobles and obsequious courtiers; but we may assume, as has been assumed by our constitutional writers, that in the interest of the Reformation this was a politic improvidence, seeing that the persons among whom the partition was made would, in accordance with the general laws of human nature, "give a readier reception to truths which made their estates more secure." Thus it came about that during many years the ordinary expenditure did not exceed the ordinary revenue of the Crown. A grant of "tonnage and poundage," and of the first fruits of benefices, was made for life to the Sovereign on his accession; and this could be supplemented on occasion by the voluntary assessments known as "benevolences." The legality of these assessments has been, and continues to be, disputed; but they were sanctioned at least by inveterate custom. So that it was only in an exceptional crisis, as when a costly war was imminent, that the Houses were summoned to impose a compulsory tax.

It would be exaggeration to assert that the judges of the high Courts of justice were corrupt; but there can be little doubt that many of them were partial to the authority by whom they were appointed, and by whom they could be dismissed. Neither the goods nor the life of any man who ventured to entertain sentiments unacceptable at Court was secure. Between heresy and treason the line was loosely drawn; and what was heresy to-day was truth to-morrow. On one hurdle six malefactors were sent by Henry to the stake,—three had denied the Catholic doctrine of trans-substantiation, three had refused to take the Anglican oath of Supremacy. The whim of the moment was the standard of right and wrong; and to that whim the most tremendous penalties were attached. The Courts of law might on occasion be unduly complaisant to the Crown; but when hard pressed they could assert their independence. There was another tribunal, however, which, as its admirers declared, was not disabled by legal scruples or troubled by legal subtleties. Short of life and death, the jurisdiction of the Star Chamber was absolute; and the members of the Star

Chamber were the Councillors of the Crown. Torture was repugnant to English notions of fair play and honest inquiry; in the Star Chamber it was freely employed. The House of Peers was another Court of criminal jurisdiction where the will of the Sovereign was paramount. Either by impeachment or Act of Attainder many of the most powerful nobles—Warwick, Suffolk, Buckingham—had been brought to the block. The Bill of Attainder was a mendacious device by which both Houses were made accessory to Henry's judicial murders. It was an instrument of gross injustice and oppression,—a suspension of legal process by an act of the legislature. The judges who had been consulted by Cromwell had declared that, although no evidence had been led, no court of law could reverse an attainder; and Cromwell himself was sentenced unheard. Whether reached by impeachment or attainder however, the goal was the same. One cannot but wonder how it should have come about, that a House of powerful and independent nobles should have been so easily satisfied of the guilt of so many of their order, especially when each new conviction added to the common peril.

While it may be true that the previous authority of Parliament was necessary for every new law, it does not appear to have been invariably obtained. Royal proclamations were frequently issued by which important constitutional changes were effected. Though the assent of the legislature was subsequently accorded, it was by proclamation that the great ecclesiastical reform was initiated. For an acute emergency it is indispensable that some discretionary power should be vested in the Crown; "what a King *by his royal power* may do" (to use Henry's words), has never been precisely determined; even democratic governments are sometimes forced to break the law, and trust to Acts of Indemnity. What may be called the reserved and latent energy of the Crown—to be exerted only when the State is in extreme peril—received under the Tudors very liberal application.

The Anglican Church as finally established under Elizabeth (at the Nag's Head Tavern, as the Catholic satirists affirmed) was a compromise. It stood midway between Rome and Geneva. The Queen herself regarded either extreme with impartial dislike. She would tolerate within her Kingdom neither Papist nor Puritan. It is probable that, of the two, Puritanism was most distasteful to her. She scoffed at Cecil and his "brothers in Christ:" yet Cecil's Puritanism was comparatively colourless and courtly. But her animosity to Puritanism could not be fully gratified. In all her Parliaments, the House of Commons, which was ceasing to be "servile," was vehemently Protestant. So were her most trusted Ministers. The early Puritans were loyal to the Monarchy—obstinately loyal to Elizabeth herself. On the other hand pretexts for Catholic persecution were easily found. Those of them who refused to take the oath of Supremacy were punished, not because they were heretics, but because they were traitors,—as no doubt many of them were, though with the majority the treason was constructive only. During the whole of Elizabeth's reign the laws against recusants were severe; but as the shadows lengthened the gloom deepened. One would have fancied that after the Armada had been dispersed, there might have been a respite. The rival Queen was dead Mary Stuart's detention in England had been, as Hallam admits, "in violation of all natural, public, and municipal law;" and her trial was a travesty of justice. But the rivalry—for an earthly crown at least—was over; and during the months of breathless suspense when the "Island Queen" was standing at bay, the Catholics had behaved well. But the Government was merciless. The rack in the Tower was seldom idle. During these last years no less than two hundred Catholics were quartered while yet alive, butchery that was justified by Bacon on the ground that "bowelling" was less painful than burning or the wheel! Hardly a protest against this cruel slaughter was heard. Lord Burleigh, indeed, who was not always consistent however, had at length in an emphatic minute which has been preserved, ventured to remonstrate:—"I account that putting to death does no way lessen them; since we find by experience that it worketh no such effect, but, like Hydra's heads, upon cutting off one, seven grow up—persecution being accounted as the badge of the Church; and, therefore, they should never have the honour to take any pretence of martyrdom in England, where the fulness of blood and greatness of heart is such that they will even for shameful things go bravely to death;" much more, he adds, when they think thus to climb to Heaven, and their obstinacy commends them to the common people who regard it as "a divine constancy." Nor should it be forgotten that when the harsh act of 1562 was passing through Parliament, Lord Montague had preferred an earnest plea for liberty of conscience, if not for liberty of speech. He entreated the Peers to consider whether it was just by penal statute to force loyal subjects of the realm "to believe the religion of Protestants on pain of death. This, I say, to be a thing most unjust; for that it is repugnant to the natural liberty of men's understanding. For understanding may be persuaded but not forced. Only a man of no courage or stomach, and void of all sense of honour, would consent to receive a new religion by compulsion, or swear the contrary of what he thinks. Even a brave man might consent to be silent—'to keep his reckoning with God alone' but to be compelled to swear to a lie, or else to die if he refused, was a thing that no man ought to suffer and endure." A fine speech for any assembly; considering the time when it was made, and the passions that were abroad, a really noble and memorable appeal.

If the Catholic was treated with merciless severity, the Puritan did not entirely escape. It is a popular superstition that persecution must fail. It does *not* fail when it is carried out with inflexible decision. It fails only when the Inquisitor is timid and irresolute. The Puritans, who were merely ejected from their livings or driven from their conventicles, rapidly increased in number, so that before the close of Elizabeth's reign a body of bitter sectaries had become formidable,—a force to be reckoned with in the political world. The Catholics, on the other hand, who had been pursued with unsparing vigour, had dwindled to a handful.

Those who write history are presumably more sagacious than those who make it. We are wise after the event. To us the folly of Elizabeth and her Ministers in their treatment of nonconformity is painfully obvious. And indeed there is good reason to believe that a little forbearance at the outset might have healed the feud. Nonconformity was in effect a protest against the Act of Supremacy and the Act of Uniformity. But the language

HENRIETTA MARIA.

From the painting in the Collection of the Earl of Buckinghamshire, at Hampden House.

of protest in the earlier years was mild. It would have been difficult no doubt at any time to have conciliated the more violent spirits who had listened while in exile to Knox or Calvin; but if a certain latitude had been admitted, if liberty of private judgment on trifles had been conceded, if reasonable elasticity instead of rigid uniformity had been the policy of Parker and Whitgift, it is possible that the discontent might have been allayed, might have died out. Then, as now, men of sense must have regarded the frivolous usages to which either party attached undue importance—the retention of a crucifix or a taper, of a tippet or a surplice, the sign of the cross in baptism, the ring in matrimony, the posture at Communion—with indifference. It was wise perhaps, when half the people were still Catholic at heart, to retain some of the ceremonies to which they had been used. The transition was more easily effected when friction was reduced to a minimum. But when it had become obvious that uniformity would occasion lasting discord, that a party (so Parsons wrote of 1594) "more vigorous than any other, most ardent, quick, bold, resolute, and having a great part of the best captains and soldiers on their side" would resist to the uttermost, a sagacious statesman would have loosened the bonds. Nor to such a Minister would the Royal Supremacy have proved an insuperable barrier. The oath might have been modified by politic reservations which would have saved the scruples of the precise. The Puritans might be, as Cecil thought, "over-squeamish and nice in their opinions, and more scrupulous than they need;" yet, by their "careful catechising and diligent preaching" they were doing service to the State, which ought rather to approve than condemn.

But it was not to be. History was to take a different course. Elizabeth was to leave the Puritan as a legacy to her successor. Even before her death he had become very truculent,—a bye-word for rudeness, asperity, and intractability. The High Commission—an ecclesiastical court armed with the powers of an Inquisition—could not silence Martin Marprelate. The Brownists grew the more they were repressed. And, as invariably happens, there was a rapid development of doctrine. The demands of the earlier dissenters were comparatively moderate,—to episcopal government in the Church, to personal rule in the State, they did not seriously object. But foolish intolerance had borne its usual fruit. Episcopacy had become hateful to them,—presbytery was not only lawful, but divinely ordained. A Government based on popular consent was the true form of civil rule. The claim for ecclesiastical independence, or rather for spiritual supremacy, was insistently preferred,—by Thomas Cartwright, at least, in language that might have been coined by Hildebrand. The civil magistrates were the nurses, but they were also the servants, of the Church; "and as they rule in the Church, so they must remember to submit themselves unto the Church, to submit their sceptres, to throw down their crowns before the Church, yea, as the prophet speaketh, 'to lick the dust off the feet of the Church.'"

It is to be noted moreover that in the later years of Elizabeth's reign, the Commons (largely reinforced from the ranks of the Puritans) clung to their ancient privileges with increasing tenacity, and were readier to assert their independence. The arbitrary exercise of the prerogative was still common. The Star Chamber continued to sit, and to inflict penalties on obstinate or contumacious jurymen. Proclamations continued to be issued. The printing of books was subjected to severe restrictions. The too rapid increase of the Metropolis was held to be a public danger, and forbidden! Once at least martial law had been proclaimed. But though the members of the Commons themselves were occasionally committed to the Tower for imprudent or insolent speech, arbitrary encroachments on their customary privileges were, in each successive Parliament, more keenly resented and more strenuously resisted. These privileges were numerous. The claim for liberty of speech and access to the royal person was preferred at the opening of each session. They were the guardians of their own order. Then the members were exempted from arrest on civil process while the House sat. They held, moreover, that they were entitled to inquire into every grievance, and to find the appropriate remedy. Before the close of the century they had attacked the subsidies demanded, and the monopolies granted, by the Crown. Elizabeth in her most formidable and autocratic

WESTMINSTER FROM THE RIVER.

From an old print by Hollar.

mood failed to overawe them. The Wentworths and their fellows were not to be silenced. Morice from his room in the Tower assured Lord Burleigh that he would continue to strive, while life lasted, for freedom of conscience, public justice, and the liberties of his country. They were warned that idle heads should not meddle with "reforming the Church and transforming the Commonwealth." But they replied that, "to utter any griefs of the Commonwealth" was theirs of right. The attack on the monopolies granted by the Sovereign to impecunious courtiers was a bitter pill for Elizabeth to stomach. The prerogative, she declared, was "the choicest flower in her garden, and the principal and head pearl in her crown and diadem." But the clamour grew so loud that she was forced to give way, and, with that politic (or feline) adroitness which she could practise on occasion, to compliment the Commons on their solicitude for the public well-being.

On every side the waters were rising. There was a pause while Elizabeth lay on her death-bed; but the storm had not spent itself. It was clear that the finest tact and the surest judgment would be needed to steer the State barque into a peaceful haven. How far the Stuarts, on whom the command now devolved, would prove fit for the duty remained to be seen.

WOOD CARVING IN DUNFERMLINE. THE BIRTHPLACE OF CHARLES I.

## CHAPTER TWO.

### THE SCOTTISH STUARTS.

The compilers of pedigrees are mainly responsible for the earlier records of the Stuarts,—what they have to tell us when they leave the region of conjecture admitting of rapid summary.

The Scottish house of Stuart was descended from the English house of Fitz-Alan, whose arms they bore, but (in allusion it is said to their hereditary office) with the fess chequy on the shield slung round the neck of the mounted knight. They were Scottish nobles for several generations before they became Scottish Kings. Many cadets of noble Norman houses came to Scotland when David I. was on the throne, and were cordially welcomed by him. Among them were two of the Fitz-Alans,—two brothers, Walter and Simon. Walter, for some reason which does not clearly appear, speedily obtained high preferment. The Steward of Scotland (otherwise the Seneschall or Dapifer) was a powerful functionary—perhaps the most powerful among the great officers of State. The office was hereditary. Conferred on Walter, son succeeded father in unbroken order, until it came to be held by that other Walter who was with Bruce at Bannockburn. He was then quite a youth; but he had already won a name by his gallant bearing and his winning manners. A few months after the great battle, he was sent to the Border to receive the Scots prisoners who had been detained in England,—among them Elizabeth the wife, and Marjory the daughter, of King Robert. His wooing must have been done while they rode from Carlisle to Edinburgh or Stirling, for early in 1315 he was married to Marjory. Next year a boy was born, but the mother died. The Steward was acting as Regent at the time,—the King being in Ireland. In 1318 he defended Berwick very gallantly against a great English army, and in 1322 he nearly surprised the English King at Biland Abbey in Yorkshire,—but for a hard ride to York, Edward would have been captured. He had had a brief, brilliant, adventurous career when in 1326 he was struck down by mortal illness. He died in his thirty-third year. "Had he lived, he might have equalled Randolph and Douglas; but his course of glory was short."

The boy who was born in 1316 was the grandson of the Victor of Bannockburn. He too was a Robert; and for thirty distracted years only the unhappy David stood between him and the throne. David, who had no love for the valiant Steward, did his best to divert the succession. But David left no son by Margaret Logie; the Scottish people would on no condition accept the English Lionel; so that on David's death the Steward's claim to the throne, under the settlement of 1318, was conceded without serious debate. It was then, however, that the rivalry of the great house of Douglas, pregnant with so many disasters to Scotland, first made itself felt,—a rivalry which a politic marriage pacified for the moment.

Robert II. was succeeded by his son, another Robert. Robert III. in spite of mental and physical infirmities, had many of the attractive traits of his family; but for some time before his death the reins of government had dropped from his hands. His younger brother, the Earl of Fife, who latterly became the famous or infamous Duke of Albany, was the real governor. Whether Albany was responsible for the death of his nephew Rothesay at Falkland is matter of controversy; that he was responsible for the prolonged detention of James in England is not open to doubt. It need not therefore, occasion any surprise that James should have regarded Albany and all his race with peculiar bitterness; and that the atonement which he exacted should have been stern and terrible.

Albany is one of those peculiar and powerful characters which perplex the historian. He had great opportunities, which he misused. Under his government, during a period of profound peace, Scotland was given over to anarchy. The patrimony of the Crown, the estates of the Church, were squandered among nobles who were little better than brigands. On the other hand, he had strong natural affections. He was a devoted father. When he sinned he sinned for his children. He appears besides to have had tastes and occupations which were uncommon in that rude society. He was a man of letters, a man of science. The contemporary annalists are his apologists. The crafty and rapacious tyrant is regarded by Bower and Wynton and Barbour with genuine enthusiasm. Amid the turbulence of Border warfare he is represented as engaged in archaeological pursuits, —recovering and restoring the relics of an earlier age. A still more striking scene has been preserved by Bower,—sitting on the ramparts of the Castle of Edinburgh, the Regent discourses to his courtiers, during the moonlight night, of the causes of eclipses and the order of the universe.

With the return of James my sketch as consecutive narrative may close; the lights and shades in the lives of the later Stuarts are familiar to us all. I turn to the question that mainly concerns us: how far their Scottish experience had fitted them for English rule. The precise relation of these Scottish Sovereigns to their people, their Parliaments, and the great feudal nobles, falls to be considered.

The Stuarts indeed had little reason to dread either the Parliament or the people. The Parliaments, through the Lords of the Articles, were easily managed; and the Commons were proud of the family who were associated with a patriotic tradition, and worthily represented King Robert. But the conflict with the aristocratic leaders was long and bitter. Feudalism died hard. Mar and March and Douglas for many a year were as powerful as the Sovereign; and in Scotland a divided rule meant anarchy. Thus it became the settled policy of the Stuarts to strengthen the authority of the Crown by reducing the power of the aristocracy. While a score of petty potentates continued to exercise an independent jurisdiction, anything like orderly government was impossible. It cannot be truly said that the Stuarts were worsted in the contest. They did much; under happier circumstances they might have done more. But the stars in their courses fought against them.

1. There was always England to reckon with. The Scots Kings had to be constantly prepared for invasion. A nation far more powerful in numbers and wealth lay on their flank. But the fighting force of the country consisted mainly of the feudal retainers of the great nobles; and when the great nobles were gravely displeased they refused to fight. Had they been cordially united they might have formed a league which would have left King and Kingdom defenceless. The utmost tact and dexterity were needed to avert a disaster which, once at least, occurred, and which more than once was imminent.

2. The Stuarts were never wealthy; and impoverished rulers are forced to husband their resources. In his anxiety to secure for himself and his family the support of the peers, the ancient revenues of the Crown had been squandered by Albany; and when James returned from his English exile he found an empty exchequer. Later on, when the abbey and other ecclesiastical lands were in the market, the Sovereign was abroad, and the patrimony of the Church was greedily appropriated by hungry nobles. The

MARRIAGE CONTRACT OF CHARLES I.

From the original document, in the Collection of Her Majesty the Queen, at Windsor Castle

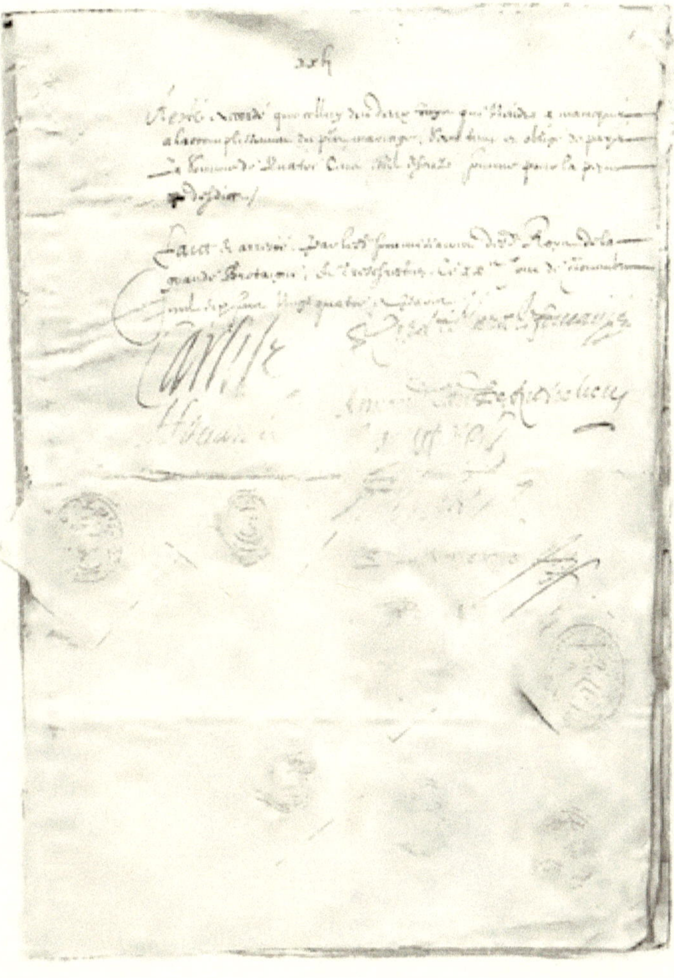
xxh

Est accordé que celluy des deux Roys qui faudra a manquer a l'accomplissement du pnt mariage, sera tenu et obligé de payer la somme de Quatre Cens Mil Escuz pour la peine du desdict.

Faict & arresté par les Commissaires desd. Roys de la Grande Bretagne; a Cambridge, le xx^e jour de Novembre mil six cens Vingt quatre.

Carlisle

league of the peers against Mary is to be ascribed, I believe, to their apprehension that she might revoke the generous grants which they had made to each other in her absence. There can be little doubt, it may be added, that Maitland of Lethington cordially approved the Stuart policy. No government, he held, could be responsible for public order so long as vast territories were under the absolute rule of a Hamilton or a Gordon.

3. It was difficult to maintain a firm and consistent policy of repression when the Sovereign was a minor: and long minorities were the curse of Scotland. Five Jameses successively occupied the throne. The first was forty-five when he was murdered at Perth,—he was succeeded by a boy of seven; the second was thirty when he was killed at Roxburgh,—he was succeeded by a boy of eight; the third was thirty-five when he was assassinated at Sauchie,—he was succeeded by a boy of sixteen; the fourth died at Flodden, aged forty-three,—he was succeeded by an infant son; the fifth died of a broken heart at Falkland,—he was succeeded by his daughter Mary who was then eight days old. We cannot wonder that in these circumstances, heavily handicapped as they were, they should have failed to keep the nobles steadily in check; the wonder is that they were able to do what they did. The surest testimony, indeed, that feudalism was on the wane, that the life had died, or was dying, out of it, is to be found in the fact that the Jameses, in spite of protracted minorities, should have been able in a manner to hold their own to the end.

4. The pre-eminence of the house of Douglas was a real misfortune for the Royal house. For more than a generation it was felt that any day a disaffected Earl, with the northern and border barons at his back, might make a bold bid for the Crown. The Stuarts and the Douglases were rival claimants; and the title of the Douglas was thought by many to be the better of the two. The Stuarts derived their title through Elizabeth More, who had been the first wife of Robert II. But her son, who afterwards became Robert III, had been born before the marriage was

solemnised. According to the Canon Law, which recognised the legitimacy of the offspring if the parents were subsequently married, the boy was the true heir; but after Elizabeth More was dead, Robert had married again, and the descendants of his second wife—Euphemia Ross—were not prepared without demur to recognise the law of succession as defined by the ecclesiastical tribunals. The Douglas derived his right through Euphemia Ross; and, whenever the conflict became acute, the superior claims of the heirs of Euphemia were obstinately preferred. There can, I suppose, be no doubt that during the reign of James II. of Scotland it was for long an open question which side would win. Had James been worsted, the Earl of Douglas was prepared to claim the Crown; and it is certain that, with two-thirds of Scotland behind him, the claim would have been admitted by the Estates.

These were obstacles to complete success,—serious obstacles no doubt; but the Stuarts themselves were to blame. I do not underrate their capacity, nor their fitness in many respects for the high place they occupied. There was hardly a member of the family who was not bright, energetic, capable. They were poets, fluent writers and speakers, adventurous soldiers, able administrators. They were resolved from first to last to hold their own; and they had a high conception of the kingly dignity; yet they were not arrogant. Easy of access, affable, quick at jest or repartee, they were ready, with a sort of plebeian audacity, to welcome good or evil fortune. They had little pride of station,—they were men and women who laughed with the keenest zest over the humours of the market-place, and who did not care to don the mask which custom prescribes when a King mixes with the crowd. The engaging address of the Stuarts attained perhaps its finest expression in Mary; but each could exert on occasion "the enchantment whereby men are bewitched." This is no more than the truth; yet the Stuart character was itself at fault. Somewhere in the metal there was a flaw. Infirm of temper, they could not bear a protracted strain; impatient of opposition, they could not play a waiting game. To form a far-reaching design, to mature it in silence, and to cling to it with dogged tenacity, was a line of policy which a Stuart might approve in his heart, but which he rarely followed. They were at once obstinate and facile,—never more so than when James IV., in spite of warning and portent, flung away his crown upon the field of Flodden. His grand-daughter had many of the fine qualities of her family; but she had also their fatal defects. She lacked the coolness, the self-control, the patience, that become the diplomatist. The quick resentment was often as imprudent as the prompt forgiveness. Her impulsive anger sometimes undid in a day the politic labour of months. Her keen contempt for the pharisaic bearing and spiritual arrogance of the "Congregation of Jesus Christ" found vent, sooner or later, in rash and scornful words that worked her infinite harm. She really desired to stand well with the English Queen; but her cousin's mean duplicity and blundering craft exhausted her patience; and a biting jest or a mocking laugh did more to exasperate Elizabeth than the Darnley murder or the Bothwell marriage.

What has now been said will serve to indicate the view I take; it would be profitless to multiply illustrations. I do not assert that their defects of temper absolutely disabled them for the work of government; but the absence of steady self-command unquestionably accounts in some measure for the ill-luck which followed them like a shadow. Their record would certainly have been less tragic had they been less impatient of counsel and control.

This then was the character, these the experiences, of the family to whom the Government of the English people had passed. It cannot be said that the omens were propitious. Apart from any other consideration, the fact that for three hundred years they had been engaged in a constant struggle for supremacy had left behind it an inevitable bias. Their aim had been to aggrandise the kingly office, to extend and strengthen the prerogative. That the immunity from criticism of a divinely appointed ruler should have become an article of the Stuart creed need not surprise us. But if this conviction should prove ingrained and ineradicable, what was to happen when they were brought into direct contact with the popular forces which were already at work in England.[1]

Nor was it less than a grave public misfortune that the present representative of the family was one who retained few of their finer traits, and in whom their foibles were caricatured. While no King could be less kingly than the Sixth James, no king was more persuaded of his divine commission. The Stuart sovereigns with rare exceptions had been poor —poor as church mice, as was said; but James was so impecunious that the very shirts he wore were borrowed. After one or two spasmodic outbursts (of which the Raid of Ruthven and the Gowrie Conspiracy may be reckoned the most audacious) the great nobles were ceasing to be troublesome; but on the other hand the arrogant bearing of the Calvinistic clergy had become intolerable. The place of the courtly and diplomatic priest of the old religion had been taken by an indiscreet and vehement minister of the new, who had no respect for decent conventions, and who rebuked King and nobles with more zeal than discretion. The English sectaries, who were separating themselves from the Anglican communion, favoured the Presbyterian rule and ritual; whereas to James, who had been preached at and prayed for all his life, the very name of "Presbyter" had become loathsome.

The character of a Stuart who combined a certain native shrewdness with boundless egotism and insatiable vanity, in whom mental irritability was as little under control as physical restlessness, has often been limned. In the collections of Calderwood and others, the testimony of his Scottish contemporaries will be found. The picture they draw almost passes belief. This egregious schoolboy, who occupies his leisure in writing a commentary on the Apocalypse, who, in public controversy swears like a trooper and scolds like a shrew (the rival theologians being "loons" and "smaiks" and "lousin knaves") is surely one of the most singular royal figures of whom any record remains. Long before he went to England, James had fallen under the sway of unworthy favourites; and among these, the Master of Gray, Francis, Earl of Bothwell, the two Campbells, one of whom, created Earl of Arran, became Chancellor of the kingdom, and married the shame-

ORDER OF ST. GEORGE.

Belonging to Charles I. From the Royal Collection.

less "Jezebel" of the Calvinistic pulpit, have attained an unenviable notoriety. The successors of Knox were prodigal of invective; neither King nor courtier was spared; and it may be admitted that James's aversion to his spiritual advisers—the Melvilles, the Lawsons, the Blacks, the Gibsons—was not without warrant. It is possible therefore, that the contemporary narratives, which come to us mainly from ministers of the Kirk, are somewhat highly coloured; yet after all, there is substantial agreement. That the only Stuart who was a grotesque and undignified pedant should have worn the Scottish Crown when the English succession opened was one of those scurvy tricks which Fortune is apt to play.

JAMES I.

From the painting by Janssen, in the Collection of the Earl of Rosebery, at Dalmeny

## CHAPTER THREE.

### KING JAMES AND THE COMMONS.

It may be said without exaggeration that all parties in England—Anglican, Puritan, Catholic—welcomed the accession of James. The waning popularity of Elizabeth partly accounts no doubt for the warmth of the greeting extended to her successor; but it is rather difficult to understand now on what grounds intelligent Englishmen could have persuaded themselves that with a Stuart prince the Golden Age was to return. The illusion did not last long. James's progress to London was slow; and before he reached the capital, the bubble had burst. Admiration, we are told, was turned into contempt. This stuttering, slovenly, ungainly Scot was not the king that had been looked for. The manners of Royalty are a factor of vital moment; and James's manners told heavily against him. The masses are not quick to recognise the solid qualities of a Sovereign, and even the classes better fitted to judge were startled by his frivolous tastes and undignified familiarity. He was in many respects shrewd and capable; but his foolish confidence in his own infallibility made him habitually indiscreet, and his pedantic learning accentuated his folly.

James who was born in the summer of 1566—a few months after the Rizzio murder—was married to Anne of Denmark in 1589. As we see him now, he is not a romantic figure; and his ardour in pursuit of Anne, who had been driven back by storm when on her way to Scotland, is rather incomprehensible. The romance indeed was short-lived. Anne's position was difficult from the first; and her judgment was often at fault. The King, to use a phrase that has become familiar, must have been "gey ill to live wi'"; and the relations between the ill-matched pair became so strained at one time that separation was imminent, and worse than separation was dreaded. But wiser counsels prevailed; and before they left Scotland in 1603 two boys were born,—Henry and Charles—Henry at Stirling on 19th February, 1594, Charles at Dunfermline on 16th November, 1600. There was also a daughter—Elizabeth, who married the Elector Palatine in 1613,—an unhappy alliance, fruitful of tragedy.

The Catholic, no less than the Anglican, was entitled to look forward with confidence to the coming of a Scottish Prince. Mary Stuart was held by the Roman Church to have laid down her life for the Faith; and James had, latterly at least, resented with not unbecoming warmth the insolent innuendoes of preachers and poetasters. The "false Duessa" of "The Faerie Queen" had been identified with Mary; and her son had insisted that Spenser should be rigorously dealt with. It may be questioned how far his zeal for her good name was prompted by genuine feeling; his sensitiveness on this occasion has been attributed to selfish regard for his own interests, inasmuch as his claim to the English

Group of 5 Miniatures

ANNE OF DENMARK, Mother of Charles I., after P. Oliver (above); HENRIETTA MARIA, after P. Oliver (right); CHARLES I., after J. Hoskins (centre); HENRIETTA MARIA, after P. Oliver (left); HENRY, PRINCE OF WALES, by Isaac Oliver (below).

From the Collection of Her Majesty the Queen, at Windsor Castle.

succession might have been prejudiced if the person through whom it came was publicly defamed. Educated though he had been in the severest school of Protestant theology, James was by nature easy and tolerant; he was ready to believe that Catholic nobles and gentlemen might be loyal subjects; and he was eager—unwisely eager, as it proved—to cultivate amicable relations with the great Catholic Powers. No pressure, I believe, could have made James a Catholic; he was too sure of his own omniscience to acknowledge any other Pope; but there was, if I may use the expression, a dominant Catholic strain in the Stuart blood, so that few of them could resist the allurements of Rome. Whatever the cause—hereditary bias or a placable temper—it is certain that the fierce animosity of his people to "the Vicar of Christ" was not shared by their King.

The Anglican parson had even surer grounds for his conviction that the new King would prove an ardent churchman. But the very considerations which reassured the Anglican should have warned the Puritan. During the early years of the century the English Puritans favoured presbytery (the Independent was of later growth); and James had had a protracted experience of Presbyterian discipline in Scotland; and, as we know, did not relish it. Elizabeth had used her influence to prejudice him against a faction whose aim, as she declared was twofold,—"to reform the Church and transform the Commonwealth." "Let me warn you," she wrote in 1590, "that there is risen both in your realm and mine a sect of perilous consequence." English sectaries had taken refuge in Scotland, where they were welcomed and entertained by their brothers in Christ. Strong language from Calvinistic pulpits had, she understood, been directed against herself. Would James allow a strange King to receive such indignity at caterpillars' hands? Let him stop their mouths or shorten their tongues; and if he would decline to harbour "the vagabond traitors and seditious inventors" who had fled from justice, she would take care that on their return they were properly handled. James responded with alacrity; the amity with England was of inestimable value; and Elizabeth's appeal could not be disregarded. The truth was that the arrogant pretensions of the Kirk had already stung him to the quick. The ministers had told him to his face that it was his duty and his privilege to consent to any act they might pass. "And why? Because the acts of the Assembly have sufficient authority from Christ, who has promised that whatever shall be agreed upon on earth by two or three convened in his name shall be ratified in Heaven; a warrant to which no temporal king or prince can lay claim; and so the acts and constitutions of the Kirk are of higher authority than those of any earthly king: yea, they should command and over-rule kings, whose greatest honour should be to be members, nursing fathers and servants to the King Christ Jesus, and his spouse and queen the Kirk." James took his revenge in the *Basilicon Doron*. The surreptitious extracts which were made from Sir James Semple's copy by Andrew Melville roused such a storm of indignation among the clergy that a public fast was proclaimed, which lasted for two days. An apostate king had become the defamer of the Kirk; and the displeasure of the Almighty could only be averted by public prayer and humiliation. It must be admitted that in the use of truculent language the preachers had met their match. Their Reformation, they were bluntly told, was the offspring of popular tumult and rebellion. Their leaders were fiery and seditious spirits who delighted to rule as *Tribuni Plebis*. They had brought about the wreck of two queens; and during a long minority had invariably placed themselves at the head of every faction which weakened and distracted the country. "Take heed therefore, my son, to such Puritans, very pests in the Church and Commonweal, whom no deserts can oblige, neither oaths nor promises bind; breathing nothing but sedition and calumnies, aspiring without measure, railing without reason; and making their own imaginations (without any warrant of the Word) the square of their conscience. I protest before the great God—and since I am here as upon my testament it is no place for me to lie in—that ye shall never find with any Highland or Border thieves greater ingratitude, and more lies, and vile perjuries, than with these fanatic spirits."

Nor was the *Basilicon Doron* his unkindest cut at the Kirk. Before he left for the South, James actually succeeded in persuading the Presbyterian Assembly to accept a modified or qualified form of episcopal rule. A seat in Parliament for each bishop or "commissioner" was the bait that he used. The proposal was bitterly resented by the leaders of the Church who, through the "bonnie buskin," saw, as they thought, "the horns of the mitre." But the King's reply was not wanting in force. "I mean not to bring in Papistical or Anglican bishops, but only that the best and wisest of the ministry should be selected by your Assembly to have a place in Council and Parliament, to sit upon their own affairs, and not to stand always at the door like poor suppliants utterly despised and disregarded."

The appeal was successful, and in spite of Ferguson's emphatic warning, "*Equo ne credite Teucri*," the Trojan horse was brought in. Conditions were attached, to prevent a too arbitrary exercise of prelatic authority, which however were not valued by those who, as Calderwood observes, seeing the danger, "considered it better to hold thieves at the door, (that they steal not) than to have an eye upon them when they have entered within the house;" and which in point of fact the bishops broke "as easily as did Samson the cords wherewith he was bound."

It was tolerably clear that from a King who had suffered as James had suffered, the Puritans had little to hope; and so it proved.

The messengers entrusted with the Millenary petition met the new King on his way to London; but consideration of its prayer (which was to the effect that uniformity in the public services of the Church should not be required) was meantime delayed. After a decent interval, a Conference, which met at Hampton Court, was summoned. James, who was in his element, presided; bishop and archbishop sat beside him; the area of the hall was reserved for the men—Puritans mainly—who vainly pleaded for relaxation. Whether, had their prayer been granted, peace would have been permanently restored may be doubted: it rather seems to me that any possible truce must have been hollow. Between Prelatist and Puritan there was a radical repugnance which could not have been healed by ceremonial change or ritual revision.

Possibly James may have been right. "No Bishop, no King," was his favourite formula. The democratic independence of presbytery was a fact not to be gainsayed; whereas, episcopacy was aristocratic and monarchical,—the distinction between the different offices, between rulers and ruled, being duly emphasised. Then the King was the head of the English Church, whereas the Presbyterian acknowledged no head but Christ. James had been taught by Elizabeth that Puritanism was seditious as well as schismatical; with his exalted notions of Kingship, he was ready to believe the worst of a system which in its devotion to republican simplicity showed no respect for dignitaries.

It is possible that a little tact might have helped to disarm hostility for the moment. But James's manner was abrupt, his language undignified and indiscreet. "If you aim at a Scottish presbytery," he exclaimed in reply to the request that they might be allowed to hold informal meetings for devotional purposes, "it agrees as well with monarchy as God and the Devil. There Jack, and Tom, and Will, and Dick, shall meet and censure me and my council. Wait, I pray you," he continued, "for seven years; then if I grow pursie and fat I may perchance hearken unto you; for that government will keep me in health, and give me exercise enough." This was the harangue which the prelates noisily applauded,—the Archbishop being satisfied indeed that "his Majesty unquestionably spoke by the special instance of God's spirit."

The Conference was followed by a meeting of convocation at which the canons of 1604 were promulgated. By these, uniformity was enforced. Rather than conform, three hundred clergymen left the Church. The secession, however, was smaller than had been looked for, and is held to indicate that the more extreme and stubborn "Sectaries" were still numerically weak. In a subsequent proclamation, James declared that having determined the matter "he would neither let any presume that his own judgment should be swayed to alteration by the frivolous suggestion of any light spirit, nor was he ignorant of the inconvenience of admitting innovation in things once settled by mature deliberation."

It is a pity when history is written in hysterics. The nice shades of

THE SECOND DUKE OF BUCKINGHAM AND HIS BROTHER.

From the painting by Sir Anthony Vandyke, in the Collection of Her Majesty the Queen, at Windsor Castle.

character and circumstance are apt to be overlooked. James, whose blustering rhetoric was a cloak for constitutional timidity, is accused (with his son) of "conspiring" against the liberties of the English people, of which the House of Commons is taken to have been the sagacious and undaunted guardian. Here as elsewhere, the intemperate partisan draws no fine distinctions—the sheep are on one hand, the goats on the other; the truth being that neither King nor Parliament was blameless. Had James been supremely sagacious, he might have recognised that a new era had come, impatient of precedent and zealous for popular rights; had the Parliament been wise they would have perceived, on more than one occasion, that, fighting for the shadow, they were letting the substance go. While it must be admitted that there was little true statesmanship in either camp, it seems to me that James adhered most closely to usage, and that on the whole his outlook was shrewder,—his homely Scotch sense indeed sometimes rising to genius.

There was a leaven of Puritanism in the Commons; and the rapid alienation of King and Parliament was probably due to the presence of men who resented James's tart treatment of their Nonconformist allies. I am not convinced that his rather crude definitions of his hereditary title to almost absolute authority, of the divine derivation of his right to rule, had much to do with the alienation. He stated it no doubt with the most unguarded directness, and in the most peremptory terms. Although a good King would frame all his actions to be according to the law, yet was he not bound by it. The absolute prerogative of the Crown was not to be disputed. "It is atheism and blasphemy to dispute what God can do; good Christians content themselves with his will revealed in his word; so it is presumption and high contempt in a subject to dispute what a King can do, or say that a King cannot do this or that; but rest in that which is the King's will revealed in his law." But Parliament, in defining his right, had itself declared that on the death of Elizabeth, "the imperial crown of the realm of England did by inherent birthright, and lawful and undoubted succession, descend and come to his most excellent Majesty as being lineally, justly, and lawfully, next and sole heir of the blood royal of this realm." The reason for the unusual emphasis of the declaration is obvious. James had no parliamentary title to the throne. The parliamentary title indeed was with the other branch of the house,—the family of his younger sister, Mary, having been preferred by Henry VIII. to the family of the elder sister, Margaret. It was necessary in consequence to fall back upon an inviolable hereditary right which no act of Parliament could disappoint. It was quite understood moreover, that James's brave words meant little,—there was no imperious and resolute Will behind them, as in the Tudor time. Though he was easy and placable by nature, he was a Stuart; and the Stuart passion sometimes mastered him. But even his passion was not impressive,—it led only to peevish outbreaks of temper which judicious flattery or a new toy could soothe. In one of his choleric moods he went down to the house at Westminster where the Commons sat, and with his own hands tore out of the Journals a "Remonstrance" which he held to be illegal. It was a grotesquely childish proceeding; a few years later it might have led to revolution; but at the moment it passed almost unnoticed. He was conscious, I think, of his weakness; and there is even a touch of pathos in his comic confession,—"I am your King; I am placed to govern you and shall answer for your errors; I am a man of flesh and blood, and have my passions and affections as other men: I pray you do not too far move me to do that which my power may tempt me unto."

The standing quarrel between James and his Parliaments related to the subsidies which, either in whole or in part, they refused to grant. Elizabeth's bequest to her successor had been a heavy burden of debt, incurred during the later years of her reign; and James himself was foolishly profuse. The ordinary revenue of the Crown had become inadequate, and the supplies that were voted were niggardly in the extreme. The King was forced to have recourse to impositions, benevolences, forced loans, increased duties, the sale of offices and honours, and other financial make-shifts,—apt to provoke hostile comment. The contention that any or all of them were plainly illegal cannot indeed be maintained. They were supported by usage, by precedent, by the decisions of the Courts of law. But the improvident parsimony of the Commons was attended with even graver consequences. The Palatinate was lost for a punctilio. No better illustration of the inconstancy of a popular assembly could be found than their proceedings with regard to the appeal for help from the Elector-Palatine, and the Protestant Princes of Germany. It is true that the King was averse to war. But if an adequate subsidy had been voted, the Commons would have divested themselves of responsibility, and any reason for hesitation on the ground of inability to provide the monies for a campaign would have been removed. It was not that they were indifferent or hostile to the appeal. When they met in spring, they came to a unanimous resolution to spend their lives and fortunes in defence of the Palatinate,—a resolution "sounded forth with the voices of them all, withal lifting up their hats in their hands so high as they could hold them, as a visible testimony of their unanimous consent, in such sort that the like had scarce ever been seen in Parliament." But the House was adjourned to the autumn; and by that time their ardour had cooled. The £70,000 that after severe pressure they voted, was a mere drop in the bucket. The loss of the Palatinate to the Protestant States was a sorry prelude to the Thirty Years' War; and had the English Commons been wisely generous, it might not have been lost.

Their temper on other occasions was far from admirable. In the negotiations for union with Scotland they showed inveterate prejudice and the narrowest jealousy. In resenting an unpalatable comment, or, as in Floyd's case, a trivial flippancy, they were positively savage. Even Hallam, the mildest critic of the lower House, is stirred to indignant protest. "The case of Floyd is an unhappy proof of the disregard that popular assemblies, when inflamed by passion, are ever apt to show for those principles of equity and moderation by which, however the sophistry of contemporary factions may set them aside, a calm judging posterity will never fail to measure their proceedings. It has contributed at least, along with several others of the same kind, to inspire me with a jealous distrust of that indefinable, uncontrollable privilege of Parliament, which has sometimes been asserted and perhaps with rather too much encouragement from those whose function it is to restrain all exorbitant power."

The general charge that James was engaged in a conspiracy against English liberty is rested mainly upon two specific allegations; (1) his decided inclination to rule without the assistance of Parliaments; and (2) his partiality for a Spanish, or, in other words, for a Catholic alliance.

Hume has asserted that though the English State had no warmer eulogist than Shakespeare, yet that the great dramatist does not once refer to "civil liberty;" and a later historian observes that the Parliament plays little or no part in the great series of historical dramas. The omission is suggestive. Up to the reign of James, the Kingship was the centre of the national life, and round it all the forces that go to make a Kingdom gathered. No hard and fast line bounded the prerogative, - it was *the King* who ruled. The meetings of Parliament were rare and uncertain. Years might elapse between the dissolution of one Parliament, and the calling of another. It has been estimated that during Elizabeth's reign the vacations were twelves times longer than the sittings. The functions of such a body were of necessity subject to strict limitations,--its share in the actual work of government could be little more than nominal. Government was a work for experts, for the King and the Councillors who had been bred to the business. A popular assembly, convened at infrequent intervals, was absolutely unfitted to discharge the high and complicated duties of imperial administration, which, even under the most democratic Constitution, must be lodged in a Cabinet or Privy Council. The English Commons, however, had the power of the purse; and, when a war with France or Spain was imminent, they were summoned to Westminster to vote the necessary supply. This, roughly speaking, was the view that prevailed when James succeeded to the Crown.

Whether this view may be approved by the doctrinaire is immaterial. The English Constitution was not fashioned by the doctrinaire. It has been a true growth, like the growth of flower or fruit. The laws of the

Medes and Persians were unalterable; but within the English Constitution there has been a happy power of adaptation. Conditions change; the imperative creed of one age is the obsolete fiction of the next. Thus the Constitution is not to be found in any written document,—usage, precedent, practice, being stronger than statute. It has had to contend age after age with novel and varied forces,—to protect itself successively against a lawless nobility, against a despotic King, against a turbulent democracy. It has once, more than once indeed, temporarily succumbed,—one day a mob of fanatics, on another a mob of soldiers, have assailed it with success. But hitherto, it has always recovered from the shock. No vital organ has been incurably hurt. It is extraordinarily tenacious of life; for its roots, oak-like, are deeply embedded in the soil from which it sprang; and thus far it has proved itself invulnerable.

The Parliaments of James, it must be admitted, would have tried the temper of a less choleric ruler. They were not only penurious in the provision they made for the public service, but they were constantly encroaching on the prerogative of the Crown. The power of making war, the right to conclude a treaty or a peace, had by immemorial usage been vested in the Sovereign. So had the disposition of the Royal family in marriage. These privileges—privileges which have never been resigned and which continue to be exercised—were invaded by the Commons. They proposed in effect to take the governing power into their own hands. It can hardly, one would think, be matter of surprise that the intercourse between James and his faithful Commons should not have been cordial; and that, as far as possible, he should have been pleased to dispense with their attendance at Westminster. There can, I think, be no doubt that the Commons were the aggressors, and that James's attitude substantially accorded with the constitutional practice and popular judgment of the time.

On the other hand, it cannot be denied that James, who, as a foreigner, had failed to gauge the intense antipathy of the English people to Spain, showed little regard for their most cherished convictions. The Puritan saw in the surplice "the rags of Popery;" the Puritan, and not the Puritan only, saw in Spain the most bitter and persistent enemy of the Reformation,—an enemy, as he believed, still powerful for evil. James did not share these prejudices, and it may be that James was right. He may have thought, reasonably enough, that the severe penal laws against recusants, which were needed when the Armada was being provisioned, might now be safely relaxed, as he may have thought, reasonably enough, that republican license was inimical to true liberty, and that Puritan asceticism, in the interest of true culture, should be restrained. It must be said for him that he bore little rancour, and that his temper was tolerant and not ungenerous. After the discovery of the Gunpowder Plot he was almost the only man in high place who kept his head. Even at that moment of extremest panic he was prompt to prefer the plea, "Do not confound the innocent with the guilty." But his Spanish policy was unwise and ill-considered. A Spanish marriage for the heir to the throne was more than the nation could stomach. To bring a Catholic Bride to England from the most Catholic house in Europe was to make terms with the Antichrist of Rome. To fancy that by a Catholic alliance the Palatinate might be recovered to Protestantism was folly. To pleasure the Spanish King by the sacrifice of Sir Walter Raleigh, the most famous Englishman of the time, was worse than folly. He might have suspected that he was being played with by the Court of Spain; and that the concessions to the Papal claims which he was prepared to make would be resented by a Protestant, and would fail to satisfy a Catholic, people.

Nor was it true that the danger to Protestantism was over. It has always appeared to me that the Reformation might have proceeded on other lines, and under other leaders, with happier results. The temper of the leading reformers was unphilosophical and unhistorical. They would hold no parley with the past; they had resolved, as Knox declared, to establish the Church of Christ *de novo*. In a work on the singularly interesting William Maitland of Lethington, I ventured to suggest that had his moderate counsels prevailed, had Knox's fanatical intemperance been effectively curbed, the Scottish Reformation might have proved more fruitful of good. Mr. Froude replied that but for Knox there might have been no Scottish Reformation—either fruitful or unfruitful;—which is possibly true. "The passions on both sides lay too deep, in my opinion, to be controlled by reason and moderation. Even now I see that actual work in the world only gets done by intense and narrow people. The water spread over the ground makes a morass; gathered into a channel, it is a running stream and drives a mill." Dr. Schaff, in like manner, has said that neither the polished culture of Erasmus, nor the gentle spirit of Melanchthon, nor the cautious measures of Cranmer, could have accomplished the mighty change in Scotland.

But if we take a wider area than Scotland, if we make Europe the unit, it would certainly seem that the policy of revolutionary violence was a mistake. I cannot help thinking that, had the conduct of the Reformation been entrusted to wiser heads and gentler spirits, the end might have been different. Had a temperate policy of Reform on the lines indicated by Erasmus been carried out, might not the whole of Christendom have been included? might not a religious truce have been concluded,—a truce which by wise guidance could have been turned into a religious peace? But the fighting men, Luther and Knox and Calvin, were preferred to Erasmus. Throughout Continental Europe the consequences were disastrous. It can hardly be questioned that the Catholic reaction was mainly due to the unreasonableness of the Reformers.

It was the rapid rally of Catholicism that made the English people uneasy. It seemed to them that the great work in which they had taken a leading part was being undone. The situation, it must be admitted, was sufficiently disquieting. Mr. Green, is, as usual, unduly and extravagantly emphatic; but there is substantial truth in his brilliant account of the triumphant recovery of Rome from the malady which for a time had been like to prove mortal. All over the Continent, the advance of Protestantism had been stayed. It had been untrue to its own first principles, and it had failed as it could not but fail. "At the death of Elizabeth, therefore, the temper of every Protestant, whether in England or abroad, was that of a man who after cherishing the hope of a crowning victory, is forced to look on at a crushing and irremediable defeat. The dream of a Reformation of the universal Church was utterly at an end. The borders of Protestantism were narrowing every day, nor was there a sign that the triumph of the Papacy was arrested."

We cannot wonder that in these circumstances the suspicion that the King's Protestantism was lukewarm, that he was ready to relax the laws against recusants, and enter into an alliance with Spain, should have alarmed the nation. James was persuaded, it may be, that only thus could the Palatinate be saved; and for the sake of argument we may assume that he had solid grounds for his persuasion. But, whatever policy was adopted, it ought to have been consistently strenuous. Whereas the King wavered from day to day. He was bound in honour and policy to aid his son-in-law; and yet he felt with acute discomfort that the Elector had invited disaster. It is possible to understand, and even to sympathise with his indecision; but the Protestant Princes were furious, and to the satirists and caricaturists of the time, the King of England was a mine of wealth. A play was acted at Brussels in which a courier brought the news that the Palatinate would be rescued without delay; powerful aid had been secured: the King of Denmark had promised to contribute a hundred thousand pickled herrings, the Dutch a hundred thousand butter boxes, the King of England a hundred thousand ambassadors. At other times he was represented with a scabbard, but without a sword, or with a sword which nobody could draw, though many were pulling at it.

Yet after all is said that can be said, James's gravest offence was his unwise prodigality to unworthy favourites. All his life he was the victim of their rapacity. The English Ambassadors to the Scottish Court had remarked upon "the vain youths and proud fools" on whom the inexperienced Sovereign lavished the scanty resources of his exchequer. Had he a million from England, they said, it would all go the same way. And so it proved. When Carr fell, Villiers rose; but extravagant provision was made for both. The finance of the Palace was reorganised under Bacon; substantial retrenchments were effected in the household expenditure; but even in his econo-

Group of 5 Miniatures:

ROBERT CARR, Earl of Somerset, after J. Hoskins *(above)*; GEORGE VILLIERS, First Duke of Buckingham, after I. Oliver *(right)*; FRANCES HOWARD, Countess of Somerset, after I. Oliver *(centre)*; JAMES STUART, Duke of Richmond, after S. Cooper *(left)*; Viscount FALKLAND, after J. Hoskins *(below)*.

From the Collection of Her Majesty the Queen, at Windsor Castle.

mies, the King was penny wise and pound foolish. Had it not been for the vast sums wasted upon greedy dependants, had he been even moderately provident, James to his dying day might have dispensed with a Parliament. On the other scandals of a dissolute Court it would be unprofitable to enlarge; but, before closing this chapter, one or two social characteristics may be noted.

There were plenty of fine wits, who could turn a rhyme very prettily, about "the town;" but in public affairs the absence of any saving sense of humour is very noticeable. No sparkle of epigram irradiates the mortal dulness. By the Puritan indeed the most harmless witticism would have been regarded as an indecorum. To him in his intense preoccupation, "life was full o' sariousness,"—the seriousness being of the sort which finds satisfaction in forcibly imposing its own uncomfortable convictions on others,—"he just never can get enuff o' fechtin." But except for an occasional bout of boisterous horseplay, the other side were quite as poorly provided. Bacon, to be sure, had the light ironical touch, and he sometimes used it to advantage. His gay wisdom could mollify even the imperious and arbitrary Elizabeth, and incline her to milder methods. It was thus that he saved Hayward from the rack. Hayward was one of the misguided people who wrote political tracts,—a practice which the Queen could not abide. "The Queen said to me that she had an opinion that there was treason in it, and asked me if I could not find any? Whereto I answered: 'For treason, sure I found none; but for felony very many;' and when Her Majesty hastily asked me: 'Wherein?' 'I told her, the author had committed very apparent theft; for he had taken most of the sentences of Cornelius Tacitus, translated them into English, and put them into his text.' And another time when the Queen could not be persuaded that it was his writing whose name was to it, but that it had some more mischievous author, and said with great indignation that she would have him racked to produce his author; I replied, 'Nay, Madam, he is a doctor, never rack his person, but rack his style; let him have pen, ink, and paper, and help of books, and be enjoined to continue the story where it breaketh off, and I will undertake, by collating the styles, to judge whether he were the author or no.'" One of James's prelates, too,—Launcelot Andrewes—could flash out at times,—winging sober counsel with wit. The two bishops, Andrewes and Neile were dining, we are told, with the King. James, with his habitual want of reserve, proposed aloud, so as to be heard by the bye-standers, the question, "Whether he might not take his subjects' money when he needed it, without the formality of a Parliament?" Neile replied, "God forbid you should not, for you are the breath of our nostrils." Andrewes declined answering as he was not skilled in parliamentary precedents; but being urged by the King, who would take no evasion, he replied ("pleasantly"), "Why then, I think Your Majesty may lawfully take my brother Neile's money; for he offers it." But from the whole political record of the time, it is barely possible to extract another jest that will pass muster. That happy persiflage which does so much, when employed by a Canning, a Disraeli, or a Balfour to lighten the dusty bye-ways of politics, was not yet in vogue;—outside the Club or the Tavern where the wits met, there was neither taste nor opportunity for brilliant trifling. The times were out of joint—not to the Puritan only. It did not need profound acumen to anticipate that the long truce would not last for ever; and even the most light-hearted may have been sobered by presentiments of coming evil. James, when he warned "Baby Charles" and "Steenie" that they would live to get their "bellyful of impeachments," must have had a shrewd guess that an age of stress and storm lay ahead.

It was, moreover, an era of transition,—in letters as in politics. The echoes of the great time were growing faint. Before the accession of Charles, most of the Elizabethans were dead. Ben Jonson (but Ben Jonson's best work had been done long before) was the one survivor of the Titans. The friend of Shakespeare was the friend of Herrick, who had supped with him at The Triple Tun and the Mermaid. A new generation was coming upon the stage. Few of the future poets were yet in their prime,—it was hard to say what forms the fresh poetic activities

might take. Meantime there was the lull that comes between one period of high imaginative inspiration, and the next. After the Elizabethan outburst, Nature needed leisure to recruit.

This was the society to which Charles, when he entered public life, was introduced, and which gave him a fairly cordial welcome. How far the greeting was sincere remained to be seen. There was an interval of peace; but the peace might be rudely broken. If the crusade for popular rights were renewed, the Commons, it might be apprehended, would find plenty of recruits. The Puritan had retired to his tent; but he was deeply displeased, and like Achilles brooded over his wrath. The sky overhead was somewhat dull and colourless; but there was a threatening light along the horizon where the cloud, big with fate,

"Was with its stored thunder labouring up."

CHARLES I RETURNING FROM SPAIN.

From the painting in the Royal Collection, at Hampton Court Palace

## CHAPTER FOUR.

### CHARLES AS PRINCE OF WALES.

CHARLES was born in 1600—he succeeded to the Crown in 1625—he was beheaded in 1649. Only half a century from first to last. When regard is had to the brief interval between his accession and his execution, we cannot but ask ourselves how it came about that, in less than five and twenty years, the decent conventions of English public life should have been exchanged for an outbreak of elemental passion, in which the whole edifice went down, the King himself, after a bloody and embittered conflict, coming to violent death. How did such stress of storm arise? Can it be said that the constitutional friction between King and Commons sufficiently accounts for this tremendous tragedy? Or were other forces at work, under the surface, of which we know comparatively little? There was no grave moral scandal among the hangers-on of the Court of which complaint could reasonably be made. There were no cruel excesses, such as the

Tudors had approved. The royal rule was mild and merciful,—the country as a whole, faring prosperously,—most prosperously when the Parliament was in retirement. There were difficulties about taxation, no doubt: but these were of old standing. Ratepayers grumble when a tax pinches: but a penny in the pound—more or less—does not lead to revolution. Religion is a fertile source of misunderstanding; but the controversies of the time were about "trifles and twelve-penny matters;" and the only people who had any real grievance were the Catholics. No martyr had been burned at Smithfield for a generation. Even if the King's word was not to be trusted, Charles was not the first King who had equivocated when in difficulties; he did not lie as Elizabeth had lied; and the punishment, in any view, was out of all proportion to the offence. How then did this tempest of passion arise,—this tempest in which an ancient monarchy and a powerful Church were wrecked? I do not think that any entirely adequate explanation has been, or can be, found. The secret has been well kept. The great civil strife of the Seventeenth Century, has an air of accident, of impromptu, of unexpectedness, which gives it a character of its own.

It may indeed be that the nation was *not* roused. It may be that the revolution was the work of a resolute and disciplined minority. Even under a republic, the majority does not always rule. The majority is commonly apathetic. It was a resolute and disciplined minority that banished the Queen of Scots. It was a resolute and disciplined minority that after the revolution of 1688 kept the Stuarts in exile. More than once by a popular franchise the exiled family would have been restored. And it is by no means impossible that the extremities of the Civil War were due to the fanatical logic of a small body of Utopian dreamers, who, in secret conclaves at home or abroad, had reburnished the weapons of Greek and Roman patriots.

Up to the day of his accession—saving of course the run to Spain—we hear comparatively little of Charles. What we do hear of him, however, is entirely to his advantage.

Charles was a delicate child,—so delicate indeed that he was not expected to live. His ankles were weak—for long he was only able to crawl on hands and knees; and, as he had inherited his father's stammer, it was with difficulty that he could make himself understood. James, who was inclined to experiment freely, in season and out of season, would have tried very drastic remedies; but, thanks to Lady Carey's sense and judgment, Charles outgrew his childish ailments. Happily for the young prince, Lady Carey, who had been made his guardian, appears to have had scant faith in doctors' drugs or the surgeon's knife: and her confidence in the *vis medicatrix naturæ* was abundantly justified. In later life Charles, who was fond of athletics, enjoyed excellent health: and he could speak on occasion readily enough, though always, I fancy, at least when excited, with a slight lisp or stammer. Mr. Gardiner, however, is of opinion that the physical weakness of his childhood left its impress upon "his tenacious and irresolute mind,"—which is possible no doubt; unless indeed the traits were hereditary, and only accentuated by a backward boyhood. He was five or six years old when Thomas Murray, a Scotsman, who was afterwards Provost of Eton, became his tutor,—from all we know a fortunate appointment. The Murrays were devoutly loyal,—none more devoutly than the daughter Anne, who, for her skilful care of the sick and wounded in the Civil War, has been compared with our Crimean Miss Nightingale. To Anne, as to half the people of England, the execution of Charles was "the greatest murder committed that ever story mentioned, except the Crucifying of our Saviour." Yet though quite out of touch with vulgar asceticism, this royalist lady was as grave and pious as any Puritan maiden,—only, as was said by one who knew her, "her piety had nothing of moroseness, or affectation, but was free and ingenuous, full of sweetness and gentleness," while "her gravity had a grace and air so taking, and agreeable, as begot both reverence and love." A pleasant picture! serving to remind us of what is sometimes forgotten by partisans, that moral seriousness was not on one side only.

The royal children were five in number, Henry, Charles, Elizabeth, and the two girls who were born in England, and who died in infancy—Mary and Sophia. The three elder were united by strong family affection. The gallant and masterful Henry was very good to his ailing brother,—"I'll make him Archbishop of Canterbury," he used to say in jest,—while his devotion to Elizabeth was unbounded. "Where is my dear sister?" were almost the last words he uttered as he lay on his death-bed. He died of typhoid fever; the fever was held to be infectious; and Elizabeth was not permitted to enter the sick room. He was not much of a student; he delighted in rough outdoor sports and pastimes, and in these he excelled; the sea was his passion: as adventurous by nature as Raleigh, he would have made an excellent sailor. Raleigh himself he admired immensely, and he deplored his long and weary captivity. "Why," he asked, "does my father keep such a bird in the cage?" There is a portrait of Prince Henry at Dalmeny; the boyish face, not untouched by a pleasant humour, is bright and animated; as we try to forecast what *might have been*, it is still possible to understand why the death of the young Ascanius cast a gloom over England.

Charles was as loyal to his sister as Henry had been. The sprightly and high-spirited girl had much of her grandmother's charm,—"the enchantment whereby men are bewitched." She made a miserable marriage; Frederic, the Elector-Palatine, was bound to fail in whatever he undertook; but Elizabeth was as staunch as steel. She was partly responsible no doubt for his evil fortune; she had urged him apparently to accept the Crown of Bohemia; but retributive justice was swift, and below the walls of Prague she was bitterly punished for any rash counsel she may have given.

The parental relations can hardly have been so close or cordial. The pleasure-loving Anne could have had little influence on her son. A thoroughly frivolous woman, she was yet a Catholic at heart,—her craving for excitement finding satisfaction sometimes in the gaieties of the Court, sometimes in the austerities of the Cloister. The contrast between James and Charles was even more marked. The boisterous familiarities of the King must have been very trying to this reserved and stately lad. The

garrulity of the father accounts in some measure, it may be, for the reticence of the son. Slow of speech and diffident in manner, Charles was no match for the good-natured but vociferous dogmatist, to whose shrewd, sound, Scottish sense he failed to do justice. The vanity of James could not have been flattered by the portraits that have come down to us; in moments of argumentative excitement—if they are at all to be trusted—he must have resembled a clamorous turkey-cock; and it need not surprise us if Charles, ashamed of his father's want of kingly restraint, should have been driven to the other extreme. He sought refuge in silence; and the habit once acquired remained with him throughout life. Suppressed irritation is like suppressed gout; and it would rather seem that Charles brooded over his wrongs. Then when the cup was full, it overflowed. Relief was found in hasty, ill-considered, and violent action. One would have fancied that the King's foolish fondness for Buckingham would have been resented by the prince. To hear James gravely warn his Council that "as Christ had his John, so he had his George," must have tried the patience of the most finished courtier. But the favourite's ascendency appears to have been absolute throughout the Palace. "Steenie" was "Baby Charles's" closest friend. The political lessons which Charles received from his father,—"That which concerns the mystery of the King's power is not lawful to be disputed, for that is to wade into the weakness of princes, and to take away the mystical reverence that belongs to them that sit in the throne of God"—were of doubtful service to him in later life; and, to a lad in his teens, the rash counsels of Buckingham must have been even more hurtful. I do not think that James ever lost his confidence in Buckingham,—though the Spanish escapade tried it sorely. Yet even in Spain, Steenie and Baby Charles were still his "sweet boys and dear venturous knights." But when the Duke returned from Madrid in angry mood, James began to weary a little of the servitude. His son he declared with petulant vehemence, was as well disposed, before he went to Spain, as any son in Europe; but now he was strangely carried away by rash and youthful counsels, and followed the humour of Buckingham, who had, he knew not how many devils within him since that journey. In one respect, if in one only, the Duke's evil example did not influence Charles. The corruption of the Court was notorious. The men were mockers and triflers, who were indifferent to decency, and to whom virtue was a bye-word. The women were as depraved as the men. From the infection of that polluted soil, and that tainted air, Charles was saved by his natural modesty. When unbecoming words were spoken in his presence, "he blushed like a girl."

"Mockers and triflers,"—yet they must have had some root of nobleness in them; for at least they could die well. Even the meaner sort held themselves bravely; while the great nobles, in the words of a biographer, "went through the trying scene with the grace and gallantry of perfect gentlemen." Lord Grey of Wilton, who had been concerned in a Raleigh or Catholic plot, when asked if he had anything to say why sentence of death should not be pronounced, replied only,—"I have nothing to say:" there he paused long; "and yet a word of Tacitus comes in my mind,—*non eadem omnibus decora*; the house of the Wiltons have spent many lives in their prince's service, and Grey cannot beg his. God send the King a long and prosperous reign, and to your Lordships all honour." And Raleigh's bearing on the scaffold was fine,—more than atoning for anything that was meretricious in his life. "I prithee," said he turning to the executioner and asking to see the axe, "let me see it; dost thou think that I am afraid of it?" He ran his finger down the edge, saying to himself: "This is sharp medicine, but it is a sound cure for all diseases." He then knelt down, and laid his head upon the block. Some one objecting that he ought to lay his face towards the east, "What matter," he replied, "how the head lies, so the heart be right?"

If Charles was backward as a boy, he must latterly have proved an apt pupil. Some of the little notes that he wrote to his father and brother have been preserved. It cannot be said that they are the letters of a precocious child; but they are prettily expressed; and they have an engaging air of sincerity and candour. "Sweet, sweet brother," he says in one, "I thank you for your letter. I will give anything that I have to you; both my horses, and my books, and my pieces, or my crossbows, or anything that you would have. Good brother, love me, and I shall ever love and serve you." Murray's office was not a sinecure; but he must have been well pleased with the progress that Charles made. James was very proud of his son's theological attainments,—which in truth were considerable. Though Puritanism was always distasteful to Charles, (and he grew harder as he grew older) he was no bigot; and if organisation, as well as individual liberty, could have been secured by other means, he would have been patient with the Nonconformists. He was not a broad churchman as Bacon was. "It is good," the great Chancellor wrote, "we return unto the ancient bonds of unity in the Church of God, which was one faith, one baptism: and not one hierarchy, one discipline; and that we observe the league of Christians as it is penned by our Saviour Christ, which is in substance of doctrine this: he that is not with us is against us; but in things indifferent and but of circumstance this: he that is not against us, is with us." But these were heights to which, at that time, few could rise, and Charles was not among the elect. Yet, like his father, he had no faith in persecution; and he would probably have fared better had he realised that the era of toleration had not arrived. He was not aware that, according to the estimate of Whig historians, it needed two centuries, or thereby, to clear the air.

Outside theology, his accomplishments were varied. He could speak with ease more than one language. He had an unusual command of French, Spanish, and Italian; and he was a fair classical scholar. He was a jurist, a mathematician. He was devoted to music of a high class; and his picture gallery was perhaps the best in Europe. There can be no question, indeed, that his taste in Art was really excellent. He was the patron of Rubens; and the great Vandykes, in many a royal gallery at home and abroad, were painted for him. The collection was scattered by Cromwell, or at least with his consent; and the nation is so much the poorer. For the great Venetian School, Charles's admiration was unstinted.

While he was King, the masterpieces of Titian and Tintoret, of Veronese and Giorgione, might be seen in England. A boorish and improvident vandalism has deprived us of priceless treasures. Yet it is fortunate that the further order of the Parliament, that all such pictures as "contained a representation of the second person of the Trinity or of the Virgin Mary, should be forthwith burnt," does not appear to have been carried out.

Charles was about the middle height. He had, we are told, a brownish complexion; his hair was of a chestnut hue; his eyes were grey. His nose was rather large,—unduly prominent, it would seem; and his forehead, though high was somewhat narrow. Browning has described him as "the man with the mild voice, and mournful eyes." The air of melancholy may have been a Vandyke convention; for his smile was winning, and his address cordial. Opinions differed widely as to his capacity. It was alleged by his enemies that he was at once rash and obstinate, as so many of the Stuarts had been: but Alexander Henderson—a witness whose evidence may be accepted without reserve—was impressed by the quickness of his intelligence, and his solid attainments. "I do declare before God and the World, whether in relation to Kirk or State, I found his Majesty the most intelligent man that ever I spoke with; as far beyond my expression as expectation. I profess that I was oftentimes astonished with the solidity and quickness of his reasons and replies—wondered how he, spending his time in sports and recreations, could have attained to so great knowledge; and must confess that I was convinced in conscience, and knew not how to give him any reasonable satisfaction; yet the sweetness of his disposition is such that whatsoever I said was well taken. I must say that I never met with any disputant of that mild and calm temper, which convinced me that such resolution and moderation could not be without an extraordinary measure of the Divine grace. I dare say if his advice had been followed, all the blood that is shed, and all the rapine that is committed, should have been prevented."

Charles, from early years, appears to have attended the debates in the House of Lords, where the oratory, when Bacon was Chancellor, was of a high order: and, even before he had come of age, the good offices of the "Prince of Wales" were constantly in request. He soothed the susceptibilities of the more truculent nobles, to whom Buckingham's mushroom-like rise was a ground of offence. When swords were like to be drawn, he kept the peace. Rutland was restrained, Southampton appeased, by the intervention of Charles. When Arundel had grossly insulted Spencer (he had declared with characteristic rudeness that Spencer's ancestors had kept sheep, while his were at the wars) the Prince persuaded the angry House to adjourn; and subsequently undertook to effect a reconciliation between the Lords. He subscribed largely to the "benevolence" that was raised for the recovery of the Palatinate; and he induced his father to remit the whipping to which the unhappy Floyd had been sentenced. So far as I have noticed, his intervention was always on the side of mercy, and in the cause of order. His judgment was sound, his attitude conciliatory, and the "discretion" of the youthful prince was universally approved. He may have been shy and silent, as we are told; but there was obviously another side to his character.

For the Quixotic expedition to the land of Don Quixote Charles was only partly to blame. What blame there was attached mainly to Gondomar and Buckingham. The Count of Gondomar was the ablest and wariest of Spanish diplomatists; yet Charles's escapade was certainly encouraged by him. But Buckingham was the moving spirit. It is said that Charles had been much impressed by a portrait of the Infanta, which was shown him in 1622. That there was a spice of romance in the adventure need not be doubted; yet a match with the sister of Philip would have had solid advantages. The pursuit of a Spanish Infanta, by an English prince, was no doubt a startling innovation in a land where innovations were forbidden. Yet if all went well the audacity of the enterprise would be forgiven. So the duke may have reasoned: and—otherwise—a holiday ride across Europe, on an amorous errand, was entirely to his taste. "If all went well." But the duke's enterprises seldom went well. Nor did this prosper.

Of the singular personality of Buckingham it is difficult to form any distinct impression. I incline to believe, however, that he has received scant justice. It could not well be otherwise. The historian who defends a man so universally detested is guilty of paradox: and paradox in an historian is the unpardonable sin. I do not suppose that Mr. Froude ever entirely recovered from his defence of Henry the Eighth. And there can be no doubt that the great nobles were right when they declared that George Villiers was "an arrogant upstart." His head was turned by his rapid rise. The son of a simple squire, he was made a Knight of the Garter before he was five and twenty. And he owed all his success, so they said, to his pretty face. Then his morals were loose—loose even for the time. "Steenie" was a sorry St. Stephen. Nor can it be denied that he was ostentatious and vain-glorious, insolent and imperious. His impatience of advice, his overweening self-confidence, led to more than one national disaster. His policy, indeed, was never more than a caprice. Such is the indictment. It is, of course, irrelevant to reply that he was never meanly avaricious, that he had no share in the bribery that prevailed, that his disposition was kindly and forgiving, that his instincts were generous. And yet it seems to me that a mistake has been made. It is a mistake to hold that he was fitted to be a royal favourite, and a royal favourite only. So far as I can judge, Buckingham was not merely the Adonis or Antinous of a corrupt Court. His manners were fascinating; but it was his high spirit that endeared him to Charles. His fair face was the beginning of his fortunes—it did not keep them. Had it not been for his want of balance, he might have made a great minister. The capacity was there. He was incompetent because he did not choose to learn, because his temper was under no control, because he was reckless and improvident. But that he was a man of great natural parts, and of really commanding ability cannot, I think, be doubted. If he grew giddy in his high place, James was to blame. If his head was turned by his rapid rise, it was the fault of the King.

Mr. Gardiner is very severe on Charles's share in the adventure.

venture to suggest—with diffidence—that the severity is excessive. Charles, if not passionately in love, was undoubtedly attracted by the Infanta. He fancied that this devout girl would make an excellent wife. She was a Catholic no doubt; and there must be mutual concessions. On the other hand his sister, to whom he was warmly attached, would reap the benefit of the alliance. She would come to her own again. Philip would insist on the restoration of the Palatinate, and Philip's word was law. So he would go to Madrid, and urge his suit in person. No one should be able to say that he was a tardy wooer. It was a bit of knight-errantry perhaps; but the risk was not too great.

The rivalry between Spain and England was of old standing. There can be no doubt that Philip was averse to the match. Whatever his ultimate attitude may have been, Olivarez, too, was for many months persistently hostile. Olivarez was Philip's most trusted and powerful Minister; and he told Charles, with perfect frankness, that Spain and Austria were ancient allies who would not quarrel over the Palatinate. They had a maxim of State, he said, that the King of Spain must never fight against the Emperor. "We cannot employ our forces against the House of Austria." "Look to it, sir," answered the Prince, "for if you hold yourself to that there is an end of all; for without this, you may not rely upon either marriage or friendship." It was mainly to save the Palatinate for his sister that Charles had hazarded so much; and now he knew that the Palatinate was as good as gone. His ardour began to cool. Yet, with the characteristic obstinacy of his race, he persevered in the chase. Marry the Infanta he would. But it could not be; dispensation or no dispensation, retreat was inevitable. The Infanta's own sentiments were well known to her friends, and were not concealed from the English envoys. Charles was "the heretic prince whose person she loathed, and whose religion she detested." These are Mr. Gardiner's words; and they supply the best apology for the "dishonourable desertion" of which the Prince was subsequently accused. If Charles's eyes were opened, before it was too late, to the light in which his suit was regarded, was he not entitled, nay bound in honour, to withdraw? He had been the dupe of the astute diplomacy of Spain, Philip and Olivarez had played a double game. Moreover he was in a false position, from which it was desirable that he should escape. He had been drawn into making concessions which it would have been difficult to keep. The English Commons were passionately intolerant; yet he had promised on their behalf to practise toleration. He had been delighted to cross the Bidassoa, and on its Spanish bank he had danced for joy; now, chilled and disenchanted, he was as eager to depart. He welcomed the admiral of the fleet that was to convoy him home as he might have welcomed an angel from Heaven. Buckingham, whose brilliant strategy had met with scant success, was profoundly chagrined. The friend of Spain became her bitterest foe, and used all his art to defame her. When the favourite's vanity was wounded, truce was impossible. Henceforth it must be war to the knife.

No time was to be lost. Eligible consorts might be found elsewhere than in Spain. James was resolved that the Prince should be suitably mated; and an embassy was forthwith despatched to Paris. Charles and Buckingham had passed through the French capital on their way to Madrid, and Henrietta Maria had been pointed out to them; but they do not appear to have been impressed. The new envoy, however, waxed warm in her praise. The day after his arrival he saw the princess,—a quick, bright-eyed girl in her fifteenth year. "My Lord," he wrote to Buckingham, "she is a lovely sweet young creature. Her growth is not great yet; but her shape is perfect." A little later he wrote to Charles that for beauty and goodness she was an angel. Charles was satisfied; and, on her side, Henrietta appears to have been nothing loath. She had seldom, Lord Kensington had been informed, put on a more cheerful countenance than that night he first saw her. "There were some that told me I might guess the cause for it." And he added that Henrietta, having borrowed a miniature of the Prince that hung about his neck, opened it with such haste as "showed a true picture of her passion, blushing in the instant of her own guiltiness."

ELIZABETH, QUEEN OF BOHEMIA.

*(Sister of Charles I.)*

From the painting by G. Honthorst, in the Collection of Her Majesty the Q
at Windsor Castle.

Personal predilections, even in royal weddings, count for something; but the French marriage was mainly a move in the great European game which was then being played. The authority of Spain as a world-wide empire might be on the wane, but she was still a Power of the first magnitude. "The proud flag of Philip waved from the Netherlands in the North over an almost uninterrupted series of fortifications, through the Palatinate, Franche Comté, the Milanese duchy, Naples, Sicily, and Sardinia, to the spot where the Pyrenees lower their crests as they sink towards the waters of the Atlantic. Behind this martial barrier was now arising once more the shadowy form of the old Empire, which had been quickened into life by the successes of Spinola and Tilly, and which was now in close alliance with the Spanish monarchy." Thus to France, lying within the monstrous coil, Spain was a constant menace: and the statesmen of France were satisfied that danger was imminent. A close alliance with England was most desirable; on what terms could it be obtained? England would have struck at Spain through the Palatinate. France, on the other hand, would have cut her line of communication with the Empire; and this could be effected by driving her from the Valteline. James for his part was ready to co-operate, so far as co-operation was practicable. What could be done to ameliorate the lot of the English Catholics, he would willingly do. But he had a Parliament to reckon with. Nor did he scruple to ally himself with a Catholic Power. He had steadily opposed a "war of religion." The Protestant States, in his view, were not strong enough to stand alone. "Protestantism could only defend itself by ceasing to be aggressive, and by appealing to the political sympathies of Catholic Powers." This, as Mr. Gardiner has pointed out, was in the main the policy which in after years crowned Richelieu with glory. To the unlucky James it brought only discredit. But Richelieu had no Parliament to reckon with.

The negotiations were protracted; the veterans of English diplomacy were no match for the great French Minister, then on the threshold of his career: and in one form or other, guarantees were exacted for which no adequate return was obtained. James as usual had the worst of the bargain,—one of the last acts of his reign. The marriage treaty was ratified on 12th of December, 1624; the King died on 27th of March, 1625. The burden of empire had grown too heavy for him.

Here we part with "the patient, much-enduring man." The historians who are most noted for the assiduity with which they polish their epigrams, and round their periods, have found a congenial subject in King James the First. Yet Scott's unstudied ease defies rivalry. The rapid pen was never at rest; there was no pause for erasure, or correction; yet how close is the texture, how robust and animated the life! "The King was deeply learned, without possessing useful knowledge; sagacious in many individual cases without having real wisdom; fond of his power, and desirous to maintain and augment it, yet willing to resign the direction of that, and of himself, to the most unworthy favourites; a big and bold assertor of his rights in words, yet one who tamely saw them trampled on in deeds; a lover of negotiations in which he was always outwitted; and one who feared war where conquest might have been easy. He was fond of his dignity, while he was perpetually degrading it by undue familiarity; capable of much public labour, yet often neglecting it for the meanest amusement; a wit, though a pedant; and a scholar, though fond of the conversation of the ignorant and uneducated. Even his timidity of temper was not uniform; and there were moments of his life, and those critical, in which he showed the spirit of his ancestors. He was laborious in trifles, and a trifler where serious labour was required; devout in his sentiments, and yet too often profane in his language; just and beneficent by nature, he yet gave way to the iniquities and oppression of others. He was penurious respecting money which he had to give from his own hand, yet inconsiderately and unboundedly profuse of that which he did not see. In a word, those good qualities which displayed themselves in particular cases and occasions, were not of a nature sufficiently firm and comprehensive to regulate his general conduct; and showing themselves as they occasionally did, only entitled James to the character bestowed on him by Sully—that he was the wisest fool in Christendom."

Henrietta Maria became Queen of England. On the 1st of May, 1625, the marriage was celebrated by proxy in front of the great west door of Notre Dame. On the 12th of June, the Queen landed at Dover, on the 16th she arrived in London. It was a dreary day; but she was warmly welcomed. The great river, which was to become the highway of the commerce of the world, was crowded from bank to bank. In spite of the rain, the omens were regarded as propitious. The rocks ahead, on which, as we know, the barque was to founder, were still under water, and invisible to the naked eye.

CHARLES I. AT GREENWICH.

From the painting by Janssen, in the Collection of Her Majesty the Qu

## CHAPTER FIVE.

### THE EARLY YEARS OF THE REIGN.

I cannot but think that the political life of Charles the First, and the political creed of which that life may be said to have been the consistent expression, may be reasonably defended. There is a good deal in the lives of most men and women that does not admit of complete justification; and Charles, though a King, was not faultless. If we insist, indeed, on regarding his political creed from the point of view of the Nineteenth Century, and with the eyes of the modern doctrinaire, we must pronounce it an anachronism, or worse. But if we try to realise what Kingship had meant up to the day when he came to the throne, and how it was regarded by men like Bacon and Cecil, we may possibly be induced to modify our conclusions.

Politics is not one of the exact sciences. An institution, a constitution, is not for all time; and the precise form it takes at any one time must depend upon the surroundings. When it is not in harmony with the contemporary necessities, with the contemporary convictions, it will fail. "It is as much a mistake to depend upon that which is true but impracticable at a certain time," Bolingbroke wrote, "as to depend on that which is neither true nor practicable at any time." The arbitrary rule of the Tudors is defended on the ground that in an age when the passion for change had grown, or had threatened to grow, anarchic, the strong hand of a Henry, or of an Elizabeth, was needed. But the same writers contend (as I understand the argument) that the authority which during an acute crisis had been lodged with the Sovereign, might, early in the Seventeenth Century have been taken from him, and restored without loss to the Commons. The royal prerogative, even when it rested on a strictly legal basis, did not require to be maintained,—might at least be safely abridged. Might be, and ought to be; for it was hostile to those popular privileges which during a revolutionary era had been temporarily resigned. The answer to this argument is simple, and need not detain us. What evidence is there to show that in the earlier years of the Seventeenth Century the lower House was qualified for imperial rule, or that it was wise to weaken the authority of the Crown? Had the prerogative been preserved intact in the hands of a capable Sovereign, who had no House of Commons to reckon with, would the Palatinate have been lost? would German Protestantism have been imperilled? Even had the crisis ceased to be acute, even had the political situation been less strained, it would have been egregious folly to have made the House of Commons, as then constituted, supreme. Mr. Gardiner says of the lower House, that "it was as yet but an incoherent mass, agitated by strong feelings, and moved by a high and sturdy patriotism, ready indeed to offer a determined resistance to every species of misgovernment, but destitute of that organization which can alone render it possible for a large deliberative assembly, without assistance from without, to carry on satisfactorily the work of legislation.'"' To Bacon, above all men, a change which should make the House of Commons master of the executive government was an object of dread; for such a change would, as he imagined, place the direction of the policy of the country in the hands of an inexperienced and undisciplined mob."

Even to-day—be it said in passing—the political opinions of thinkers like Bacon and Cecil are not to be treated with disrespect. "Confidence," said Chatham, "is a plant of slow growth in an aged bosom." It might be well were the modern schools of political thought less confident than they are. The claim made by James to be an "absolute" ruler rouses a storm of indignant protest; whereas the claim of the House of Commons to "absolute" rule is freely and cheerfully accorded. But absolute power, wherever lodged, is a grave political danger. Whether the danger is greater when it is lodged with a King than when it is lodged in a popular assembly, is at most only a question of degree. There is the risk of hasty and ill-considered action, which may eventually end in disaster, in either case; but an elective body, unused to restraint and the sober traditions of office, is more liable to be moved by passion or panic. The danger was foreseen, and more or less guarded against, by the founders of the Swiss and American republics; but the check of the Referendum is unknown to our Constitution; and a scratch vote of the House of Commons may at any moment lead to evils that cannot be repaired.

Nor can it be admitted that under the Tudors there was a virtual suspension of the Constitution. The Golden Age, when the prerogative was severely limited, and popular rights were freely recognised, is, it may be feared, an "idol" of the imagination. There could be no dispute about the methods employed by the Tudors; but the plea that these methods were inconsistent with earlier usage, has seldom been approved by experts.

The great jurists of the Seventeenth Century, from Bacon onwards, were satisfied that the plea was untenable. Our most recent historians (with the exception of the hysterical) are of a like mind. Mr. Gardiner, for instance, is ready to admit that there was no firm ground on which it could be rested. Discussing the debate on the power of the Crown to levy "impositions," he observes: "It is impossible to read the arguments without perceiving that all the speakers agreed in attributing to the constitution of the thirteenth and fourteenth centuries far more of a settled character than it in reality possessed. They all seem to have imagined that on important points there was some fixed rule to which all had assented, the contravention of which was known to be a breach of constitutional law. They failed to seize the true character of the epoch as a time of struggle, during which the idea of law was gradually evolving itself in the midst of a conflict of opposing wills."

But there is a class of political reasoners who are prepared to hold that politics *is* an exact science, and that what is good to-day must have been good yesterday and the day before. Charles and his councillors are to be judged by an immutable law, which does not admit of empirical modification, and applies as truly to the Seventeenth Century as to the Nineteenth. It is thus that Mr. Green eulogises the political insight of Pym: "He saw that as an element of constitutional life Parliament was of higher value than the Crown; he saw, too, that in Parliament itself the one essential part was the House of Commons. On these two facts he based his whole policy in the contest which followed. When Charles refused to act with the Parliament, Pym treated the refusal as a temporary abdication on the part of the Sovereign, which vested the executive power in the two Houses, until new arrangements were made. When the Lords obstructed public business, he warned them that obstruction would only force the Commons 'to save the Kingdom alone.' Revolutionary as these principles seemed at the time, they have both been recognised as bases of our constitution since the days of Pym. The first principle was established by the Convention and Parliament which followed

on the departure of James the Second; the second by the acknowledgment on all sides since the Reform Bill of 1832 that the government of the country is really in the hands of the House of Commons, and can only be carried on by Ministers who represent the majority of that House." To number the fallacies which such reasoning involves would require a separate treatise; here it is enough to say that historical justice cannot be administered by men in whom the habit of mind which takes no count of times and seasons has become chronic. The bases of the Constitution! The Constitution had no such bases. Of course when the King abdicates, the executive government, as matter of necessity or expediency, is carried on by the other branches of the legislature; but neither formally nor virtually had Charles abdicated, and no precedent sanctioned the parliamentary *usurpation*. Nor can it be said that by any maxim of the Constitution, by any statute or usage, had the government of the country been vested at any time in the House of Commons. It is true that *since 1832* we have had a government more or less democratic, a government which through the House of Commons fairly reflects the mood of the majority; but it is no less true that during nine-tenths of our history the Commons were of no account, and that in point of fact the country was governed by the Sovereign or by the Lords. Up to 1832, it was only during brief periods of civic strife, when the Constitution was in abeyance, that the Commons could be regarded as more powerful than the King, or as powerful as the Lords. They were in name and fact the lower House,—a subordinate branch of the legislature.

In weighing the wisdom or want of wisdom of Charles, these are considerations which are too frequently neglected. It is right that we should endeavour to understand for what, from their own point of view, the Stuarts were fighting. They were fighting, on the one hand, as they fancied, to preserve the monarchy from democratic invasion; they were fighting, on the other, to restrain Puritanic excess. It was a defensive war—not a war of aggression. The share in the government of the country which had belonged to their predecessors was being taken from them. The needful supplies were refused by the Commons in order to extort concessions from the Sovereign. *That* was revolution. Then it was impossible to reconcile the claim of a morose and fanatical sect to spiritual independence and the control of the conscience, with the supremacy of a national Church and the genial traditions of an ancient society. Anything was better than anarchy; but if the Puritan prevailed, anarchy was imminent. The reasoning may have been faulty—as it no doubt was in a measure. But it was not so unsound as it is sometimes held to have been. The general aim was sound enough—had it been pursued with discretion. As time went on the contest became more embittered; and then neither side would listen to reason—neither Roundhead nor Cavalier.

A brilliant and suggestive writer has said that "to recognise a period of transformation when it comes, and to adapt themselves honestly and rationally to its laws, is perhaps the nearest approach to perfection of which men and nations are capable." Of this recognition, of this adaptation, neither Roundhead nor Cavalier was capable. The Cavalier clung with unreflecting tenacity to the past; the *Civitas Dei* of the Roundhead was a dream.

We shall see, as we proceed, how far it can be fairly argued that the popular party was acting only "in defence." The royalist statesmen and soldiers were of another mind. After his bloody victory over Argyle in Lochaber, Montrose wrote to Charles. The letter was one of many, not wanting in political wisdom, in which he urged the King to make no treaty with the rebels. "Your Majesty may remember how much you said you were convinced I was in the right in my opinion of them. The more Your Majesty grants, the more will be asked; and I have too much reason to know that they will not rest satisfied with less than making Your Majesty a King of Straw." A King of Straw! The words are strong; yet it can hardly be doubted that in the main Montrose was right. From the beginning of the conflict the Kingship, as the true centre of national life, was in peril. Later on there was no disguise. It was the conviction that there was no half-way house on the road the Parliament was taking—nothing between it and chaos—that made Falkland a Royalist, a tardy and reluctant Royalist. Even Charles was better than military rule and a dictator.

In his conflict with Puritanism, Charles was worsted. But in Puritanism itself there was no element of permanence. Whatever was distinctive, whatever was truly characteristic, in the Puritan theology, in the Puritan rule of conduct, has ceased to be credible to moderately reasonable men. The "moral seriousness" of Puritanism is shared by all devout souls to whatever communion they belong. Whenever we get "purity without excess of rigour," "gravity without fanaticism," we are beyond the ring-fence of Puritanism. It was not its moral seriousness, it was its narrow severity, its furious dogmatism, its Judaic exclusiveness, its asperity, its acerbity, its ignorance of the spirit, its bondage to the letter, of Holy Writ, its morose protest against lawful and wholesome mirth, the excessive importance it attached to "trifles and twelve-penny matters," finding for instance in the innocent lawn sleeves of the bishop "Romish rags and the mark of the beast"—it was these that gave it an individuality, a life of its own. Consequently it was bound to fail. A system that is to endure must be founded on the radical facts of human nature. But Puritanism took no count of a large part of human nature. It dwarfed the imagination; it cramped the intellect. There could have been no true national development on Puritan lines.

Yet even to-day Puritanism does not lack defenders. Mr. Green selects Colonel Hutchinson and John Milton, and commends them to us as representative Puritans. He fails to see that in their better moods they were not representative,—that they only become admirable when they cease to be Puritanic. It is when Colonel Hutchinson rises into a finer and sweeter air that his intrinsic charm asserts itself; Milton would have been an incomparably greater poet had he left his polemics behind him. Take "Lycidas" for example, and compare the poet with the Puritan.

Here is the poet :—

"For we were nursed upon the self-same hill,
Fed the same flock, by fountain, shade, and rill.
Together both, ere the high lawns appear'd
Under the opening eyelids of the Morn,
We drove a-field, and both together heard
What time the gray-fly winds her sultry horn,
Battening our flocks with the fresh dews of night,
Oft till the star that rose at evening bright
Toward heaven's descent had sloped his westering wheel."

Here is the Puritan :—

"What recks it them? What need they? They are sped,
And, when they list, their lean and flashy songs
Grate on their scrannel pipes of wretched straw;
The hungry sheep look up and are not fed,
But, swoln with wind and the rank mist they draw,
Rot inwardly, and foul contagion spread;
Besides what the grim wolf with privy paw
Daily devours apace, and nothing said."

Which is best? Or take his prose. Do we prefer the strenuous moralist who is not content to cherish "a fugitive and cloistered virtue, unexercised and unbreathed, that never sallies out and seeks her adversary, but slinks out of the race where that immortal garland is to be run for, not without dust and heat," to the envenomed controversialist who, as M. Scherer says, "replied to Morus and Salmasius by reproaching them with the wages they have taken, and with the servant-girls they have debauched?" Both in his poetry and his prose, Milton is only at his best when he forgets that he is a Puritan.

Lord Macaulay may have given too keen an edge to his irony when he observed that the Puritan hated bear-baiting not because it gave pain to the bear, but because it gave pleasure to the spectators; but Charles Kingsley, in the characteristic paper on "Plays and Puritans," where he essayed to prove that the modern life of England had been profoundly modified by Puritanism, shoots even wider of the mark. How did the Puritan regard the Play? Just as he regarded a Greek statue, a painted

Madonna, a Gothic chapel. They were all vanities of the flesh, coming between the soul and God. Stephen Gosson, denouncing poets, painters, players, sculptors, as "caterpillars of the Commonwealth," maintained that there was a graduated scale of declension,—"from pyping to playing, from playing to pleasure, from pleasure to slouth, from slouth to sleepe, from sleepe to sinne, from sinne to death, from death to the devil;" and William Prynne recommended that actors should be sent to the House of Correction, set in stocks, and whipped, "and if they still persist in playing after these corrections, they may be burned with a hot-burning iron, of the bredth of an English shilling, with a great Roman R on the left shoulder, which letter shall remain there as the perpetual mark of a Rogue; and if this will not reforme them they may be banished, and after, if they return again and persist incorrigible, be executed as felons." Who would listen to such folly to-day?

No,—a creed of this sectarian complexion had no future. It was inevitable that, on a wider and truer estimate of man's spiritual life, the characteristic limitations of Puritanism should be discarded. There are episodes no doubt in its annals which still appeal to us—at times. But if ever the attitude of the Puritan rouses our sympathy, it is when he ceases to be arrogantly egotistical and vindictively virtuous; and becomes, amid the hardships of a prison, or in the loneliness of exile, a pathetically human figure. "So they left that goodly and pleasant city which had been their resting-place near twelve years; but they knew they were pilgrims, and looked not much on those things, but lift up their eyes to the heavens, their dearest country, and quieted their spirits."

I resume the narrative.

The twenty-five years following the accession of Charles are crowded with events of first-rate importance both at home and abroad. In a rapid sketch like the present, Continental politics must be treated with the utmost brevity. We know that for thirty miserable years there was continual conflict among the States of Europe. Before the conflict was ended the balance of power had shifted. The authority of Spain had been persistently on the wane, while France under Richelieu had become the dominant Power. England had been mainly, if not exclusively, occupied with her own troubles; and her statesmen failed to recognise that in the interval the map of Europe had been altered, and that our relations with the different Powers required to be readjusted. Cromwell's vigour in the conduct of foreign affairs has been extravagantly lauded; but Bolingbroke's indictment of a policy which encouraged the ambition, and lent itself to the aggrandisement, of France, has been approved by later writers.

The course of the political conflict in England would be more instructive could it be regarded as proceeding on the normal lines of constitutional development. It may be that for some years after the accession of Charles, this character was (or seemed to be) preserved. But, later on, the conflict became abnormal; and becoming abnormal it became—not uninteresting, for the interest never flagged, but—comparatively uninstructive. It is difficult to say when the orderly flow of the current was interrupted, and turned as a destructive flood into an alien channel. On no chart has the exact point of departure been marked. But from a general survey we may, I think, reasonably conclude, that there were three recognisable stages in the progress of the conflict;—the first, when it was well within the lines of the Constitution; the second, when it had ceased to be conducted with prudent regard for constitutional precedent; the third, when it involved an appeal to arms and the ruthless logic of civil war. Throughout the whole conflict, Charles was the central figure; and his death marked its close.

"I am ready to depart," the dying Sir Henry Saville is reported to have said, "the rather that having lived in good times, I foresee worse." And it was thought of evil augury at the time that the Bishop of Carlisle should have selected for the Coronation sermon the text from Revelation,—"Be thou faithful unto death, and I will give thee a crown of life." But in the shout of welcome with which the nation greeted the new King, any discordant note was drowned. From that welcome even the Popish princess,—"nimble and black-eyed, brown-haired, and, in a word, a brave lady"—was not excluded. The amity—unhappily—was short-lived.

Buckingham, as usual, was the disturbing element. One after the other, his enterprises proved abortive. A succession of brilliant victories was to add lustre to the new reign, and bring the Commons to reason. But they would not come off. Fate, as he held, was perverse. In the Netherlands, before Cadiz, at Rochelle, the bodies of thousands of honest English peasants were left to rot. But it was not the malice of fortune that was to blame; it was the incurable levity of the heaven-born Minister. During four years the Duke was at the helm; and they were four years of disaster for England and for Charles.

It is fortunate that we need not follow this Will-of-the-wisp in his erratic career. It is enough to say that failure succeeded failure with exasperating monotony. Had the Duke been the only victim, there would have been small cause for regret; but the King himself was gravely compromised. It is hard to say how many of his subsequent misfortunes are to be traced to his obstinate loyalty to Buckingham.

The mood of the Commons when they met did not make for peace. The first Parliament of Charles did not differ appreciably from the last Parliament of James. One wonders at times whether these Parliaments accurately reflected the temper of the people. It would rather seem that from defective electoral arrangements the hostile Puritan element was unduly favoured; and that a franchise on a wider basis—a franchise which did not largely exclude the agricultural occupier—would have secured a fairer representation. It is not to be denied at least that, on more than one occasion, while the Commons were profoundly stirred, the nation remained not only tranquil, but apathetic. The talking went on at Westminster; and to Westminster the agitation was confined. Had there been any strong public feeling on the subject of parliamentary privilege, the penal dissolution of the popular assembly would hardly have been allowed to pass without protest. But, so far as we can judge now, neither prolonged recess nor penal dissolution occasioned the smallest anxiety.

Bacon's view of the functions of the lower House had met apparently with ready and general acquiescence.

The first act of the Commons was distinctly aggressive. The permanent revenue of the Crown was mainly derived from a grant known as "tonnage and poundage" which was voted at the beginning of each reign. The grant had hitherto been made for life; and—so far—the Sovereign had been rendered independent of Parliament. It was by tonnage and poundage that the Royal state was maintained; and a resolution to withdraw or reduce the grant would constitute a breach of a solemn parliamentary compact. But the Commons were not to be deterred by modern precedent or ancient usage: the King must be taught that they had the power of the purse: that no action could be taken without their consent: and that in the event of the prerogative being exercised in a manner of which they disapproved, supply would be refused. So tonnage and poundage was granted for one year only.

The Bill, limiting the grant to one year, did not pass the Lords: and the duties continued to be levied by the officers of the Crown without serious remonstrance. The conviction that tonnage and poundage formed part of the hereditary revenue, and that the parliamentary vote was a matter of form, was too strong and general to be shaken. A "subsidy," however, could only be granted by Parliament; and in view of the obligations contracted by the State (mainly at the instance of the Commons) Charles confidently expected that his request for an ample supply would be favourably entertained. He was too sanguine. Only two subsidies, amounting in all to about £112,000, were offered. Such an offer could hardly be regarded as serious; it was rather, as Hume has observed, "a cruel mockery" of the young King.

Charles, however, was not discouraged. When the Houses met at Oxford, he instructed his Minister of Finance to renew the application. Ample explanations were given. The King himself, in simple but touching language, added his appeal. His whole revenue had been already exhausted in the public service. He was without means even for the daily subsis-

tence of himself and his Household. This was the first request he had made; he was young and at the commencement of his reign; if he now met with kind and dutiful usage it would endear the Parliament to him, and preserve a perfect accord between him and his people.

But the Commons had hardened their hearts. They remained inexorable. A Continental conflict conducted by Buckingham was not to their taste; and so long as they disapproved of the policy of the war, no further supply would be granted. If it was true that the King was in pecuniary straits, he would be the readier to listen to reason. They were not unwisely or sordidly parsimonious: they were acting solely for the public interest. So they said.

If the Commons were prepared to give little, they were ready to take much. Their zeal for Protestantism was tempered by a hearty disrelish for religious liberty. The freedom of the conscience for which they contended was the freedom to make others think as they thought. While they were content as yet to conform to the Anglican ritual, they were resolved that only one construction should be placed upon the Anglican articles. No toleration of course could be extended to the Romish Antichrist. So long as the Papacy was politically dangerous, the law against recusants must continue to be vigorously enforced. But there was as little toleration for the Arminian rector as for the Catholic priest. Calvinism was to be stereotyped. A sound belief in the doctrine of eternal election was to be made compulsory by statute; and any deviation from the narrow path which Calvin trod would be punished by fine and imprisonment.

It could occasion no surprise that that party in the English Church which was represented by Laud and Montague (and which was favoured by Charles) should have incurred the hostility of the Commons. It was Arminian in doctrine; in ceremony it was ritualistic. The mark of the beast was upon it. Human reason, in deference to human frailty, had ventured to modify the Divine decrees. The priest, with symbolic rites borrowed from Paganism, had come between the soul and God. The evidence on which these broad propositions were rested was often incredibly trivial. When he writes of the more precise Puritan, it is with difficulty that Hume veils his scorn. "Some men of the greatest parts and most extensive knowledge that the nation at this time produced could not enjoy any peace of mind, because obliged to hear prayers offered up to the Divinity by a priest covered with a white linen vestment." It is true that Laud and Montague and Mainwaring were in quite another fashion just as narrow. If the communion-table was not placed by the eastern wall, if the officiating functionary did not wear a surplice, if there was any link wanting in "the slippery chain of episcopal anointments," the validity of the service, through which the grace of God was to be conveyed to the penitent, was seriously imperilled. The secular critic will regard the fanatical intemperance of either sect with a smile; but no ridicule will avail to alter human nature; and, till the end of time, men who are in deadly earnest will find a bone of contention in the merest trifle. Laud was in deadly earnest, —as were Pym and Eliot. In the meantime no doubt it was the Calvinistic Commons who were eager to visit erroneous opinions regarding the mysteries of religion with legislative pains and penalties. Nonconformity in doctrine was denounced by nonconformists. Dissenters insisted that there should be no dissent.

The abrupt dissolution of a Parliament where such views prevailed could not be regretted. The Commons were in an impracticable mood. They would have rendered all government impossible, except on their own terms. The situation, no doubt, was novel. The line between the executive and legislative functions had not yet been clearly drawn—nor was it drawn till a much later period. Until the uncertainty was resolved, friction was inevitable.

Charles succeeded to the throne in the spring of 1625; and before the close of 1629 three Parliaments had been summoned, and three had been dissolved. Three Parliaments in four years meant—could only mean that the gulf between the King and Commons had widened. The incidents varied; but the spirit was the same. Until grievances were redressed, the King must wait. The Commons would make no provision for the Crown unless their demands were first complied with. They would extort concessions by refusing supply. *That* was the policy which, in each of the Parliaments, the popular leaders thought fit to adopt. How far their policy was justifiable depends of course on the nature of the claims that were preferred by them. The question in certain aspects is one of constitutional law only; but it will be better to discuss it on broader grounds. Was the conduct of the Commons reasonable or unreasonable? Were their leaders prudent, moderate, conciliatory, just? Did they show any aptitude for rule? If storm arose, could they steer the vessel into port? If the crew proved mutinous, could they restore order?

Religion was likely to play the leading part in the years that were coming; and the attitude of the Houses to religion was not reassuring. The proscription of certain theological opinions was not a task that a lay assembly should have been eager to undertake. It may be admitted that they had considerable provocation. Foolish books on the passive obedience due to the King were written, and foolish sermons were preached by the Arminian clergy. The illustrations were often as grotesque as the argument. In one of the earlier homilies it is pointed out that the Virgin Mary obeyed the proclamation of Augustus to go to Bethlehem. "The obedience of this most noble and most virtuous lady to a foreign and pagan prince doth well teach us, who in comparison of her are both base and vile, what ready obedience we do owe to our natural and gracious Sovereign." Jerusalem—Laud had told the Parliament in effect—is builded as a city that is compact together only when this ready obedience is secured. The same doctrine had been laboriously inculcated by Montague, Mainwaring, and others of the party which gathered round Laud. The sermons were extremely silly; it was folly to write them; but it was worse than folly to punish the writers by fine and imprisonment. The intolerance of the Commons was possibly in some respects more marked than the intolerance of the clergy. From one point of view, indeed, Laud and his friends might be regarded as the liberal churchmen of the time: they were averse to controversy on the mysteries of religion; so long as men led blameless lives, discussion was to be avoided rather than encouraged. Though the Commons did not win much credit by their incursions into theological territory, yet symptoms of deeply-seated spiritual disorder (however grotesque) are not to be treated with cynical ridicule; and Hume reflected only the rather shallow and scoffing mood of his generation when he wrote,—"To impartial spectators, surely, if any such had been in England at that time, it must have given great entertainment to see a popular assembly, inflamed with faction and enthusiasm, pretend to discuss questions to which the greatest philosophers, in the tranquillity of retreat, had never hitherto been able to find any satisfactory solution."

Nor does it appear to me that the action of these Parliaments in delaying to provide adequate supply can be commended. It prevented Charles from carrying out his engagements with the Protestant Powers of the North. The results were disastrous, permanently disastrous, for Protestantism. Gustavus Adolphus was wise in time; but battle after battle was lost by Christian of Denmark and his allies; and the plains of Northern Germany were overrun, and its cities pillaged, by the mercenaries of Tilly and Wallenstein, because the English Commons—occupied in wringing concessions from their young King—had failed to provide him with the sinews of war.

That the encroachments of the Commons were being pushed too far for the public safety, is now seldom disputed. The House was seriously displeased when Coke and Carew refused to disclose the confidential communications that had passed between them as Councillors of the Crown. No one now dreams of invading the privacy of the Cabinet; for it is well understood that government could not be carried on were State secrets less jealously guarded. The responsibility of Ministers to Parliament was an entirely novel doctrine when Charles came to the throne,—one for which neither King nor people were prepared; and it need occasion little surprise that an extreme application of the doctrine should have been strenuously and successfully resisted.

The Petition of Right was the sole legislative achievement of which these Parliaments could boast. It was in substance a declaratory statute; but it did not take statutory form. Its exact effect as an explanation of the law gave rise to much legal argument. It sought to restrain the prerogative in so far as "arbitrary" arrest and "arbitrary" taxation were involved; but it may be doubted how far it succeeded. Could the King imprison a subject without stating on the warrant the cause of imprisonment? The more the question was agitated, the more embarrassing it became. It was admitted on all sides that there were cases where it was in the public interest that no cause should be assigned. How were such cases to be dealt with? Lord Bristol suggested that the King had a regal as well as a legal power; and a resolution to that effect was adopted by the Lords. But the assertion of a reserved sovereign power was not agreeable to the Commons. The King was never above the law, —the prerogative when validly exercised was part of the law. The subtlety hardly deserved the prolonged discussions to which it gave rise. The King was not acting outside the law when he exercised a discretionary power approved by the law. Wherever a discretionary power has been accorded, the exercise of the discretion is necessarily a legal act; and the only question that may possibly arise is as to the limits within which the discretion may be validly exercised. The difficulty was ultimately solved or evaded by a declaration, to which both Houses agreed, that the Act was not to be regarded as encroaching on the prerogative. But if the prerogative was left intact, where was the use of the Act?

It cannot be said that the last scene of the parliamentary play reflected any credit on the performers. Eliot, against the advice of Pym, whose parliamentary tact was unrivalled, had committed the House in Rolle's case to a line of action which would have conferred an undue privilege upon those of its members who were engaged in trade; and he desired that, before the adjournment, which was imminent, took place, certain resolutions which he had prepared should be read and approved. The

Speaker refused to put them on the ground that they were not relevant to the question before the House, and rose from the chair. He was promptly seized by Holles and Valentine, and pushed back into his seat, where he was forcibly detained. The tumult that followed was obstinate and prolonged. The authority of Eliot was invoked: he was a consenting party; but the Speaker was firm, and the resolutions were not put from the Chair. They were ultimately read by a member amid approving clamour; and then the door was unlocked, and the members were permitted to depart. There is no more shameful incident in our parliamentary annals. It is to be regretted that the last day of Eliot's last Parliament should have been stained by such excesses. We must all agree with Mr. Gardiner that, if the preponderance in the Constitution was to pass from the King to the House of Commons, many a compensating change would be needed before the great alteration could be safely effected.

With the exception of Sir John Eliot and Sir Thomas Wentworth, none of the leaders of these short-lived Parliaments attained permanent distinction. The true career of the great Yorkshireman belongs to a later period (as does that of Pym); here it is enough to say that the contrast between the manly and vigorous common-sense of Wentworth and the somewhat frothy vehemence of Eliot can hardly have been appreciated by the members.

Sir John Eliot was the first parliamentary "martyr." He was undoubtedly a man of real distinction—a simple and high-minded English gentleman; but the praise lavished on him has been somewhat excessive. He had the temperament of the orator, and it was only as an orator that he excelled. The oratorical temperament does not appear to consist with strict veracity,—consciously or unconsciously, it seeks to mystify and mislead. It is always in an extreme of heat or cold; and its passionate panegyric is as extravagant as its fierce invective. An oration of the first class should have backbone,—eloquence is only consummate when it is reasoned eloquence. Selden hit the nail on the head when he said, "rhetoric without logic is like a tree with leaves and blossoms, but no root." So far as it is possible to judge from the fragments that have come down to us, Eliot's oratory, though impressive at the moment, was crude, laboured, and involved. And he was moreover profoundly unfair. The invective against Buckingham is simply outrageous. The great satirists are careful to introduce redeeming traits; an air of judicial reserve, while softening the acrimony, adds to the weight of the censure. But there is no light or shade in the hateful "Sejanus" of Eliot's inflamed imagination. On the other hand, the panegyric is just as immoderate. He had a profound belief in the perfect wisdom of a Parliament which would not tolerate any show of intellectual dissent, which clamoured for persecution, and whose parsimony let loose the dogs of war—Spinola, Tilly and Wallenstein—on the unoffending Protestants of the North. Of that assembly he spoke with bated breath, in language from which Dryden might have borrowed his eulogy of Rome:—

"A milk-white hind, immortal and unchanged,
Fed on the lawns, and in the forest ranged;
Without unspotted; innocent within;
She fear'd no danger, for she knew no sin:
Yet had she oft been chas'd with horns and hounds,
And Scythian shafts, and many winged wounds
Aim'd at her heart; was often forc'd to fly,
And doom'd to death, though fated not to die."

From the denunciation of Buckingham, I might select more than one salient passage. Possibly the most characteristic is that in which the orator compares Charles's Minister with the Sejanus of Tacitus, who was "*audax; sui obtegens, in alios criminator; juxta adulatio et superbia;*" but it is too long to quote. One other parallel he drew before he sat down. "I will conclude with a particular censure given on the Bishop of Ely in the time of Richard I. That prelate had the King's treasures at his command, and had luxuriously abused them. His obscure kindred were married to earls, barons, and others of great rank and place. No man's business could be done without his help. He would not suffer the King's Council to advise in the highest affairs of State. He gave *ignotis personis et obscuris* the custody of castles and great trusts. He ascended to such a height of insolence and pride that he ceased to be fit for characters of mercy. And therefore, says the record of which I now hold the original, *per totam insulam publice proclametur. Pereat qui perdere cuncta festinat; opprimatur ne omnes opprimat.*"

"If the duke is Sejanus," Charles is reported to have said, "I must be Tiberius." And he dissolved the Parliament.

Nor can it be forgotten that it was the ferocious invective of Eliot and the Commons that turned Felton's head. They had denounced Buckingham as a public enemy—the enemy of God and man. On the poor, weak, muddled brain of the unhappy fanatic their wild words fell like liquid fire. So he bought a tenpenny knife, went down to Portsmouth, and with one well-directed blow avenged his country's wrongs, and his own.

It is a pity that Charles did not comply with Eliot's last request—to be allowed to die by the Cornish sea. Even his emaciated body might not be moved to where "upon the beachèd verge of the salt flood" his kindred rest. The denunciation of Buckingham was never forgiven by a King who was not prompt to forget.

The attitude of Charles to the Parliaments which Eliot led has not been approved by the historians of the time. Their animadversions, it seems to me, are somewhat ungenerous. Charles often acted from impulse; and the impulse--both in word and deed—was often unwise. So much may be admitted. The Commons, however, tried him severely. On more than one occasion he went down to the House, and lectured them as his father had lectured them. "Mr. Speaker, here is much time spent in inquiring into grievances. I would have more time bestowed in preventing and redressing them." Not that he questioned their right to consider grievances. "But, for God's sake, do not hazard the ruin of my prerogative and your liberties by overmuch consideration." But any schooling was sure to be resented by them—as it was. The arrest of Eliot and Digges, for words spoken in the House, was arrant folly. But the insinuation that Buckingham.

HENRIETTA, DUCHESS OF ORLEANS

*(Youngest Daughter of Charles I.)*

From the painting by ~~Sir Peter Lely~~, in the Collection of Her Maj[esty]
at Buckingham Palace.

to please King Charles, had poisoned King James was monstrous; and Charles's indignation was natural. The frequent dissolutions did him no good; and his emphatic "Not a minute!" proved that on one occasion at least he would not listen to prudent counsel. All this may be admitted,—Charles was at once impulsive and obstinate. But the graver charges are ill-supported. On what do the persistent accusations of bad faith, of "perfidy," rest? Mainly on his conduct while the Petition of Right was under consideration. Various incidents in connection with its parliamentary fortunes are said to reflect discredit on Charles. A bill avowedly introduced to restrain the exercise of the ancient prerogatives of the Crown cannot, it is true, have been regarded with much favour by the King. But there is no proof that he meant to disregard its provisions. I have already commented upon the Act in connection with the practice of arbitrary arrest. It was also directed against the practice of arbitrary taxation. Yet, in spite of the Act, export and import duties—"tonnage and poundage"—continued to be levied by the officers of the Crown. This, it is contended, was an evasion of its provisions by Charles and his advisers. But Mr. Gardiner's argument that these duties—"the King's dues"—were intentionally, if not expressly, excluded from its operation, is unanswerable *. Then it is contended that the form in which the royal

* "Nor was it only in his resolution to leave the interpretation of the laws to the judges that Charles took ground which was at least formally defensible. That the words of the Petition of Right, praying that 'no man hereafter be compelled to make or yield any gift, loan, benevolence, tax, or such like charge, without common consent by Act of Parliament,' ought to have covered the case of customs duties is a proposition from which few would now be inclined to dissent. Yet amongst the words used, only 'tax' was sufficiently general to be supposed for a moment to cover the case of duties upon imports and exports, and even that word, though often used loosely to apply to payments of every kind, had the specific meaning of direct payments, and in this sense would not be at all applicable to the dues which were levied at the ports. When, therefore, Charles said that in granting the petition he had never intended to yield on this point, he undoubtedly said nothing less than the truth. He might have said even more than he did. It is as certain as anything can well be that, either because they did not wish to enhance the difficulty of obtaining a satisfactory answer from the King, or because they expected to gain their object in another way, the Commons never had any intention to include the question of tonnage and poundage in the Petition of Right. The Tonnage and Poundage Bill had been brought in early in the session. From time to time it had been mentioned, but, except a few words from Phelips, nothing had been said to give it any sort of prominence. What would have been easier than, by the addition of one or two expressions to the petition, to include the levy of these duties amongst the grievances of the House? Yet nothing of the kind was done, though the words of the petition, as was known to every lawyer, if not to every member of the House, were such as would be acknowledged by the King to cover the case of tonnage and poundage. What was still more important was that the Petition of Right, like every other statute, was subject to the interpretation of the judges, and that it was well known that the judges were in the habit of deciding every doubtful point in favour of the Crown. It was therefore with full knowledge that the ambiguous word 'tax' would not carry with it the consequences which they now wished to derive from it, that the framers of the petition, themselves being lawyers of the highest eminence, had abstained from strengthening their work with other words which would have put an end to all doubt. For these reasons, the insertion of the appeal to the Petition of Right in the final Remonstrance can only be regarded as a daring attempt to take up new ground which would place the right of the House above that decision given in the last reign by the Court of Exchequer, which they had hitherto contested in vain." (Gardiner Vol. VI., p. 326.)

consent was originally accorded was unprecedented. So it was; but the form of the Act was unprecedented. It was not an Act; it was a Petition to the King; and the King answered accordingly. "The King willeth that right be done according to the laws and customs of the realm; and that the Statutes be put in due execution, that his subjects may have no cause to complain of any wrongs or oppressions contrary to their just rights and liberties, to the preservation whereof he holds himself in conscience, as well as obliged of his prerogative."

Then it was that the clamour arose. The Commons were in a state of preternatural suspicion. Assent, it was asserted, had not been validly given. The usual words in the old Norman French had been purposely omitted; it can only be said that in view of the form and terms of the Petition their omission was natural, and that the omission, if it was an omission, was rectified without delay. Charles went down to the House next week, and informed the Parliament that the former answer had been duly considered. "But," he went on, "to avoid all ambiguous interpretations, and to show you that there is no doubleness in my meaning, I am willing to please you in words as well as in substance." Then at his request the Petition was read again, and the Clerk pronounced the old words of approval,—"*Soit droit fait comme est désiré.*"

There were shouts of applause, and a few more words from the King. "This I am sure is full; yet no more than I granted on my first answer; for my meaning was to confirm all your liberties; knowing, according to your own protestations, that you do not mean to hurt my prerogative. And I assure you that my maxim is that the people's liberties strengthen the King's prerogative, and that the King's prerogative is to defend the people's liberties. You see how ready I am to satisfy your demands; so that I have done my part; wherefore if the Parliament have not a happy conclusion, the sin is yours; I am free from it."

The Parliament had *not* a happy conclusion—as we have seen. On whom the blame rested may be matter for argument. The conflict in the meantime was to cease. The situation had grown intolerable. The con-

CHARLES I DINING IN PUBLIC.

From the painting by Van Bassen, in the Royal Collection, at Hampton Court Palace

stant friction had worried the King and wearied the people. The temptation to lock the doors of the House was irresistible. The experiment was tried—not without success for a time. The early years of personal government were coincident with a season of peace and prosperity. How long the truce might have lasted, had rational counsels prevailed, we cannot tell. We are apt to blame Laud for driving the ship on the rocks. But knowing what we know now of the spiritual pains that, ere men in the prime of manhood had grown old, were to tear England asunder, we may possibly conclude that the force of the hostile current would have baffled the most expert pilot.

## CHAPTER SIX.

### PERSONAL RULE.

There could no longer be any doubt as to the attitude of the Commons. Their claim had been explicitly stated. The powers which had hitherto been vested in the Sovereign were to be transferred to them. By them the patrimony of the Crown was to be administered. By them the policy of the State was to be determined. By them responsible ministers were to be appointed; by them responsible ministers were to be removed.

Mr. Matthew Arnold, in a passage to which I have adverted in a previous chapter, has observed with characteristic lucidity that to recognise a period of transformation when it comes, and to adapt themselves honestly and rationally to its laws, is perhaps the nearest approach to perfection of which men and nations are capable. By "transformation" is meant in effect the transfer of power from one body to another. The transfer is sometimes peacefully effected. At times indeed it comes "without observation," so that no formal deed of conveyance is needed. On the other hand the struggle between the two bodies is often protracted and severe. The severity of the conflict will vary according to circumstances. A complete mistake may have been made. The strength of the respective forces may have been miscalculated. The time may not be ripe. The demands preferred by the one body may be studiously moderate, or extravagant and excessive. True political insight, or wilful and unreasoning obstinacy, may account for the resistance of the other. And so on. There is no general law to which appeal can be made,—except possibly that the party in possession may be presumed to have the better title. Those who assail must show cause; on them the onus rests.

The Commons in this instance were the assailants. Their case was that the time had come when by a normal law of development the effective power of the State should pass from the King to the people. It seems to me that Charles was entitled (possibly bound) to resist. Resistance, however stubborn, could not be regarded as "frivolous or vexatious." The King had fair ground for holding that he was not bound to divest himself of the ancient rights and attributes of sovereignty. He was entitled at least to try the question. Had he succeeded in repulsing the assault, the natural conclusion would have been that the claim (to say the least) had been preferred prematurely, and that the conditions under which the transfer could be properly effected were not present. It will be admitted that nothing is gained for true progress by premature action. So far as one can judge from the events that followed, the claim of the Commons was not only premature, but excessive. They were not prepared for predominant rule, far less for absolute. When the leap in the dark was taken, it failed. Except as a warning, the revolutionary movement was futile. The Revolution of 1688 proceeded upon other lines. The Utopias of political dreamers were thrust aside. Experience had been gained, and (then and later) the experience was utilised. The evolution of popular rule was found to be a very gradual process,—a process not to be forced. Freedom broadened slowly down from precedent to precedent.

The Royalist historian, on the other hand, need not hesitate to admit that the conduct of the defence was often open to observation. Some of the measures to which Charles was compelled to resort were of doubtful legality. The wisdom of patience was not always recognised. The attempt to overawe the House by the arrest of its leaders was as bad a blunder as Flodden. Yet a beleaguered force must sometimes take the offensive. They become aggressive in self-defence. The sally is a recognised method of raising a siege. It is occasionally successful. The Royalist was more loyal to the Constitution than the Roundhead; moderate men of all parties had gathered, were gathering, round the old flag; and, but for Cromwell and his Ironsides, Charles might have won. A divinity still hedged the King; and there were scores of sturdy yeomen in every county who, had time served, would have taken to heart the warning of Melantius:—

> "Think what thou dost; I dare as much as Valour;
> But 'tis the King, the King, the King, Amintor,
> With whom thou fightest."

I have ventured to express a doubt whether the nation at large took any lively interest in the feuds between Charles and his Parliaments. The truce that followed the dissolution of 1629, and in which all parties appeared to acquiesce, accentuates the doubt. No Parliament was summoned for eleven years. During the first six or seven years we search in vain for any indication of widespread discord or discontent. Wise men ask themselves if there can ever be any adequate cause for revolution; and it is true that in many cases the movement is from the frying-pan to the fire; but even where there is no distinct or palpable grievance, the desire for change sooner or later makes itself felt. "Sooner or *later*," and Charles may easily have persuaded himself in 1630 that any agitation there had been had died down; and that the peace that England, alone among the nations, was enjoying would last his time. It was, as it proved, a "devout imagination;" yet we may well believe that these years—say, from 1629 to 1636—were the brightest of his life. The fine lines of Dryden on the return of Charles II :—

> "Henceforth a series of new time began,
> The mighty years in long procession ran,
> Once more the God-like David was restored
> And willing nations knew their lawful lord."

might have been applied by sanguine royalists to Charles I. when he escaped from his parliamentary servitude. Unhappily for the Stuarts, the "long procession"—in the one case as in the other—came to a premature close.

His history of this period is, for many pages, headed by Mr. Green, "The Tyranny." One seeks in vain for anything in Charles's conduct which justifies the insistent use of so strong a word. The odious acts,—the oppression, the cruelty, the crime—which are associated with the memory of tyrannical rulers are, on this occasion, conspicuous by their absence. The Parliament did not meet, and tonnage and poundage continued to be levied. If liberty consists in the exercise of the electoral franchise, liberty in that sense was crippled. But during the six or seven years to which I refer political prosecutions were well-nigh unknown, and no Puritan was seriously molested on account of his faith. Although, in spite of Milton's pregnant plea, the liberty of unlicensed printing was not to be conceded for many years, no tribunal sought to interfere with the liberty of private judgment. Much has been made of the proceedings against Prynne in the Star Chamber for the publication of "Histriomastrix." But the complaint proves that there was little or nothing in the ordinary administration of the law with which fault could reasonably be found. One swallow does not make a summer; and even if Prynne's punishment had been indefensible, it would be ridiculous to base a general charge upon a solitary indiscretion. According to the view of the time, however, the punishment was not indefensible—quite the reverse. Had Prynne written against the Commons as he was held to have written against the Queen, his head—and not his ears only—might have been in peril. Mr. Carlyle admits that the book is entirely unreadable,—densely

CHARLES I AND HENRIETTA MARIA.

From the painting by Daniel Mytens, in the Collection of Her Majesty the Queen, at Buckingham Palace.

stupid as well as profoundly foolish. *We* punish the writer of a silly book by declining to buy it; but then (as Mr. Carlyle insists) our methods are less "heroic" than those of our ancestors.

Within the past twenty or thirty years, the materials out of which "history" is composed have enormously increased, and the difficulty of selection is correspondingly enhanced. When we go further back, and examine for instance the authorities on which David Hume relied, we are struck by their apparent, and indeed absolute, paucity. It is impossible to read his History of England in a critical spirit without discovering that there is seldom a page on which an inaccuracy, more or less trifling, more or less serious, may not be detected. But if we take the narrative as a whole, it is curious how little the general outlook has changed. He belonged to a particular school of political thought, and for that allowance must be made. To him, Puritanism (instead of being as to Carlyle a devout heroism) was simply an eccentricity. But due allowance being made, how bold is the outline, how vigorous the point of view! This boldness and vigour we have failed to retain. We know so much now that any fearlessness of judgment, any breadth of handling, is simply impossible. The accumulated mass of matter is fairly bewildering. Hume said that Cromwell was "a fanatical hypocrite." Whoever said so to-day would be ostracised. We pause; we hesitate; our dissent is tentative; our assent provisional. Among a host of conflicting witnesses, we have ceased to be confident.

These considerations must occur to anyone who, out of the documents recently made public, attempts to construct a reasonable and consistent portrait of Charles the First. The conventional language of blame, no doubt, is still in use; his silence, his indirect dealing, his bad faith, continue to be denounced. On the other hand the martyr of the thirtieth of January (though the service has been discontinued) is still a prominent figure in the High Church Calendar. Yet it is singular how ill the denunciation fits in, how little the eulogy agrees, with the facts as now ascertained.

> "Treason doth never prosper. What's the reason?
> Why:—if it prosper, none dare call it Treason."

Nothing succeeds like success; whereas failure is heavily handicapped. The documents, for instance, going to show that injustice has been done to the man or woman who has lost, are frequently not forthcoming. There can be no doubt that Mary Stuart's good name suffered in public estimation for more than a century from the mutilation or suppression of inconvenient papers. Charles has also suffered,—though possibly more from carelessness than from deliberate design. We now know all that is likely to be known; and it appears that he was neither the saint nor the sinner of popular repute, and that the unreasoning eulogy, the unreasoning invective, are alike wide of the mark.

Difficult as the task has become, we must try, before getting into the thick of the political conflict, to figure to ourselves how Charles stood, how England stood, about the year 1630.

So far as I understand his character, Charles—"the man with the mild voice and mournful eyes"—wanted that buoyant and elastic habit of mind which is so useful to public men engaged in great affairs. There is an ebb and flow in the tide of human fortune; a public man must be prepared for reverses; but reverses are of two kinds, temporary and permanent. The course of true policy does not always run smooth. A great enterprise indeed seldom comes to a fortunate issue without a check. If the check is only accidental and superficial, the boat will right itself in time; but it may be vital, and mean total wreck. A really great statesman will in either event preserve his equanimity; and ever, like the wise Ulysses, "with a frolic welcome take the thunder and the sunshine." He will not allow himself to be unduly depressed; but will apply his mind with cheerful alacrity to consider the position in all its bearings. If the obstacles are insuperable he will retire; if they are not he will press on, and probably win in the end. This was not the spirit in which Charles worked. He was easily moved, and, acting on impulse, did not weigh the difficulties that confronted him till it was too late. Unsustained by a naturally buoyant temperament, he was readily discouraged; the molehill became a mountain; and the result in many cases was premature and undignified retreat. The retreat was not unfrequently conducted with an ill grace; he hung back; then suddenly gave way; and "swearing he would ne'er consent, consented." But he was not always facile; sometimes he shut his eyes and his ears; would not listen to friendly remonstrance, would not see the gulf before him; would risk all on a cast of the dice; in short, was obstinate at the wrong time.

I do not think he need be judged by his foreign policy. It is really no disparagement of him to say that he failed to find his way through the labyrinth of Continental politics. Had it not been for his sister and her children, he would have had no foreign policy; had it not been for the Palatinate, he would have followed Wentworth's advice, and devoted himself to internal reform. Upon the whole, seeing that the Commons would vote no sufficient supply, the wiser policy would have been to abstain altogether from intrigues that in the absence of adequate force must necessarily be futile.

Though rash and impetuous where his feelings were concerned, his mind worked slowly and laboriously. The quickness and vivacity of intellectual movement, so characteristic of many of the Stuarts, had not been included among the gifts which his fairy godmother had bestowed on Charles. He could not adapt himself to unaccustomed conditions; they bewildered him; with leisure he might have recognised the signs of the times; but he had no chart to guide him, and his steering was wild. Ill-at-ease in a great crisis, we need not wonder that the charge of shifty insincerity should have been brought against him. It was not insincerity; it was irresolution—the irresolution of a ruler from whom the rapidly rising tide had hidden the ancient landmarks.

In his first skirmish with the Commons, the King may be said to have won; and during the long truce that followed, there was peace at home and abroad. Charles's conception of kingly duty may have been erroneous; but at least he tried hard to act up to it. His Court was moral, frugal, abstemious. There were to be found at Whitehall witty and brilliant women, like Lady Carlisle, the friend of Pym, the friend of Strafford; poets and artists and statesmen; but no excess was tolerated; and the social life, if possibly a little dull and angular, was dignified and decorous. The King was now happy in his domestic relations. The death of Buckingham had cleared the air. Henrietta Maria belonged to a nation of coquettes; but coquetry was her worst fault. She had the piquant charm of the Frenchwoman. Charles, having heard that she was small for her age, was surprised on the day they first met to find her so tall,—"up to his shoulder." Fancying that she might wear high-heeled shoes he glanced at her feet, whereupon drawing her skirt aside she exclaimed, "Oh! c'est bien à moi, je ne porte pas de mules, et ne suis ni plus haute ni plus petite." She was little more than a child when she was married, and for some years she behaved like a spoilt child. Upon the whole Charles acted wisely and well. He took the right method. The French Catholics who had come with her were the cause of the mischief; and in spite of treaties and entreaties the French Catholics were dismissed. Until Bassompierre was sent over to counsel her, there were constant bickerings, which did not entirely cease while Buckingham was alive. Then Charles's patient tenderness was rewarded. Henrietta became the most loyal and affectionate of wives. She acquired an ascendency which she retained to the end,—not perhaps always to her husband's advantage. But black-eyed, sprightly, vivacious, frolicsome, she was just the woman to charm away Charles's darker mood, to soften into graciousness that shy and sensitive reserve. Then children were born to them,—the charming group who live on the canvas of Vandyke. A group for whom strange fortunes were in store! Charles, Prince of Wales, James, Duke of York, Henrietta, Duchess of Orléans, Mary, Princess of Orange, the Princess Elizabeth, and the young Duke of Gloucester,—quaint little men and women who were to learn that even for princes life is no holiday pastime.

Charles had very considerable capacity for business, and he was one of the most methodical of men. The minutes of the great departments which he corrected with his own hand (for he was fastidious and even finical in the use of words) have been preserved. For several years, aided by the penurious but indefatigable Weston (latterly Earl of Portland), he

was his own Minister. But soon after Buckingham's death, two new men appeared at the Council board. The one was Wentworth, the great Earl of Strafford; the other was Laud, who was to be Archbishop of Canterbury. They were then, and ever afterwards, the closest allies, the most trusted councillors, of the King. It was a hard fate that brought three such men to the block. Nothing, I think, proves more plainly that Parliament was as yet unfit for the great part it had undertaken to play, than its virulent vindictiveness in shedding innocent blood.

Wentworth was one of the men on whom the "grand air" sat as of birthright. In whatever he did there was the note of distinction. He was born to rule. He drew his power to govern men from the two qualities that are said to distinguish the poetry of Byron--sincerity and strength. Absolutely destitute of affectation, never thinking of effect, he impressed by his simple directness. His "Thorough" has been wilfully misunderstood; it meant only—Whatever thou doest, do with thy might. The impression that he was violent, that he made his way by sheer force, is due to the same misunderstanding. There is the force of brute rage which is merely destructive. The wild elephant simply crushes the obstacles in its path. But though the born ruler goes as directly to his goal, his progress is due as much to persuasive tact as to strength. In all true rulers, as in Strafford, there is the magnetic force which draws rather than drives. He is reputed to have been stern; he is accused of overbearing imperiousness; there was the Swiftian frown on his brow, his hands were rough as Esau's. So it was said; but the grave, austere, masterful man had a flood of tenderness in his heart. When his children are about him, he is as playful as a boy. "Little Mrs. Ann,"—little Mrs. Ann is four years old—is the most capable of stewards, gravely superintending in papa's absence the building of the new house at York; "she complained to me very much of two rainy days, which, as she said, hindered her from coming down, and the building from going up, because she was enforced to keep her chamber and could not overlook the workmen." Politicians too often use the Church for their own purposes; their homage is hollow; but Wentworth was a sincere and humble believer. His foreign policy was one of peace,—he would have nothing to do with adventures at Cadiz or Rochelle. His domestic policy was one of reform,—the poor were no longer to be ground down by the great: their miserable hovels were to be repaired, their scanty earnings protected. Had he lived in our time he would possibly have represented the Democratic Tory. But he had no faith in the House of Commons as then constituted. He held with Bacon that it was a mob with no cohesive force or executive capacity. That this mob should pretend to govern was an impertinence; and he regarded with dismay the irreconcilable and encroaching spirit of the popular leaders. Wentworth in England, Montrose in Scotland—and the sentiment of romantic and chivalrous loyalty was strong in both—used the same language. "They will never rest till they have made you a King of Straw!" So Montrose wrote to Charles: and Wentworth wrote to Carlisle,—"You best know, my Lord, how much the regal power has become infirm by the easy way such have found who with rough hands have laid hold upon the flowers of it, and with unequal and swaggering paces have trampled upon the rights of the Crown, and how necessary examples are (as well for the subject as the Sovereign) to retain licentious spirits within the bounds of sober humility and fear. In the meantime," he adds, "none of those clamours or other apprehensions shall shake me, or cause me to decline my master's honour and service, thereby to soothe these popular frantic humours; and if I miscarry this way, I shall not even be found either so indulgent to myself, or so narrow-hearted towards my master, as to think myself too good to die for him."

From servitude to the Commons Wentworth would have saved the King, by adhering unreservedly to a policy which made him financially independent of parliamentary aid. There was to be no revolution; recent Parliaments had been intractable; but the mood would pass. When they had ceased to sulk, a fresh Parliament might be called. But it must be wisely guided, as his own Irish Parliaments had been guided. There must be the velvet glove as well as the iron hand. It really seemed at one time as if his sanguine augury had been sound. The Parliament that met in 1640 was substantially loyal,—willing and anxious, indeed, for amity with the King. But—as we shall see—the treachery of Vane spoilt all.

Wherever Wentworth was invested with large powers, his determined and dauntless spirit made itself felt. His administrative genius, moreover, was of the highest order. He was President of the Northern Council at York, and Lord Deputy of Ireland. The great Yorkshire families were still mainly Catholic, and the recusants were numerous and powerful. Then, as ever, Ireland was "the house of misrule." In either case a keen intellect and a strong will were needed. Both were found in Wentworth; and while the disaffected Yorkshiremen were kept in due order, a season of firm and fearless rule in Ireland changed the face of the island.

As sincere as Wentworth, but far less discreet, William Laud was an eminently dangerous adviser, especially to a man like Charles. The King had a passion for orderly conformity to formal law, and Laud ministered to this passion. The rich diversity of individual temperament—so characteristic of Shakespeare's countrymen—was viewed by both with cold disfavour. The erratic was to be religiously avoided. Within the National Church (and no other was to be tolerated) the strictest discipline must be maintained. Laud did not become Archbishop till 1633; and while Abbot was alive Laud's authority was confined to his own diocese, and his insistence on ceremonial unity was not seriously or widely resented. It was not indeed until the suspicion that he was at heart a Papist became general that the Puritan public took alarm. No suspicion could be more unfounded. It was not to the doctrine or ritual of Rome that he inclined,—it was to the doctrine and ritual of the primitive Church. But the Puritan theologian could not be brought to see the difference, which in truth is somewhat microscopical. The imprudence of exciting such a suspicion in the England of the Seventeenth Century ought to have been obvious. Even to-day the Nonconformist is satisfied that the High Church is a station on the road to Rome. If such suspicion is still possible, we need not wonder that the precise Puritan of 1633, who looked on the Pope as Antichrist and Rome as a more corrupt Babylon, should have felt uneasy.

Abbot died on August 4th, 1633, and two days afterwards Charles greeted the Bishop of London with the words: "My Lord Grace of Canterbury, you are very welcome." "The little meddling hocus-pocus," as Williams called him, was henceforth to work (profoundly confident that he was doing God service) irreparable mischief. His judgment on Charles that he was a "mild and gracious prince, who knows not how to be, or to be made, great," has so far stood the test of time. But it may be safely added that, had it not been for Laud, the mild and gracious prince might have died in his bed.

But neither Wentworth nor Laud could be held to represent the highest culture of the time. It was in the society that gathered round Lord Falkland at Great Tew near Oxford that the wisest and most moderate thinkers of the Seventeenth Century were to be found. That open house looked like the University itself,—so many scholars coming thither "to study in a better air." Falkland himself was the ideal gentleman,—"wearing the white flower of a blameless life" through an age of stress and storm. He was dear to England, and to him England was dear; and when in a well-nigh unaccountable paroxysm the fertile English fields were deluged with English blood, it broke his heart. "From the entrance into this unnatural war, his natural cheerfulness and vivacity grew clouded and a kind of sadness and dejection of spirit stole upon him, which he had never been used to." Later on "those indispositions which had before touched him grew into a perfect habit of uncheerfulness; and he who had been so exactly easy and affable to all men, became on a sudden less communicable; and thence very sad, pale, and exceedingly affected with the spleen. When there was any overture or hope of peace, he would be more erect and vigorous, and exceedingly solicitous to press anything which he thought would promote it; and sitting among his friends often after a deep silence and frequent sighs would, with a shrill and sad accent, ingeminate the word, *Peace, Peace*; and would passionately profess that the very agony of the war, and the view of the calamities the kingdom did and must endure, took his sleep from him, and would shortly break his heart."

Yet, like the Apostle of the Gentiles, Falkland had few natural advantages, his bodily presence was weak, and his speech contemptible. But the unclouded soul irradiated the body; and to the inner ear of scholar, philosopher or poet the harsh voice was musical as is Apollo's lute. "That little person and small stature was quickly found to contain a great heart, a courage so keen and a nature so fearless that no composition of the strongest limbs and most harmonious and proportioned presence and strength ever more disposed any man to the greatest enterprise; it being his greatest weakness to be too solicitous for such adventures. And that untuned tongue and voice easily discovered itself to be supplied and governed by a mind and understanding so excellent, that the wit and weight of all he said carried another kind of admiration in it, and even another kind of acceptation from the persons present, than any ornament of delivery could reasonably promise itself, or is usually attended with. And his disposition and nature was so gentle and obliging, so much delighted in courtesy, kindness, and generosity, that all mankind could not but admire and love him."

These are the words of Lord Clarendon, who never writes of his early friend without rising into an "ampler ether." "The Lord Falkland," he says elsewhere, "was wonderfully beloved by all who knew him, as a man of Excellent Parts, of a Wit so Sharp, and a Nature so Sincere, *that nothing could be more Lovely.*" Recent writers—Principal Tulloch, Mr. Matthew Arnold—have been hardly less tenderly appreciative. The reader who desires to join the notable company who met at Great Tew must turn to Principal Tulloch's fine and animated work on rational theology in England in the Seventeenth Century—a book that ought to have many readers; but the close of Mr. Arnold's eloge on "the martyr of sweetness and light, of lucidity of mind and largeness of temper"—is too characteristic to be omitted. "Let us bid him farewell, not with compassion for him and not with excuses, but in confidence and pride. Slowly, very slowly, his ideal of lucidity of mind and largeness of temper conquers; but it conquers. In the end it will prevail; only we must have patience. The day will come when this nation shall be renewed by it. But, O lime-trees of Tew, and quiet Oxfordshire field-banks where the first violets are even now raising their heads!—how often, ere that day arrive for Englishmen, shall your renewal be seen!"

We hear little of the leaders of the Opposition during these years. Pym, the great parliamentary strategist, by whom the defection of Wentworth had been bitterly resented, was biding his time. Eliot was dying in prison,—a fine, rash, impulsive, magnanimous man. The prison life does not appear to have been severe; one is glad to know that he saw his friends, and that he could "take the air" when so inclined. But the spring months of 1632 were ungenial; he felt the cold; and preferred to remain indoors. Though a few of the rank and file may have nursed their wrath to keep it warm, the numbers of the disaffected rapidly fell. The royalist camp was crowded, while the rebel army melted away. The mercantile class was quickly conciliated,—trade was brisk, and, in spite of tonnage and poundage, fortunes were to be made. Then the lawyers came in,—as was natural,—the claim of the House of Commons to over-ride the Courts of Law being regarded by them with disfavour. To the cursory observer—and not to the cursory observer only—it might well have seemed that the pacification was complete.

During these years—1631-1635—a member of the last Parliament, who as yet had taken little part in public affairs, but who was to become widely notable, was farming or brewing at St. Ives. Of Oliver Cromwell at his grazing farm on the Slepe Hall estate, Mr. Carlyle writes: "A studious imagination may sufficiently construct the figure of his equable life in those years. Diligent grass-farming; mowing, milking, cattle-marketing; add 'hypochondria;' fits of the blackness of darkness, with glances of the brightness of very Heaven; prayer, religious reading and meditation; household epochs, joys and cares:—we have a solid substantial inoffensive Farmer of St. Ives, hoping to walk with integrity and humble devout diligence through this world; and, by his Maker's infinite mercy, to escape destruction, and find eternal salvation, in wider Divine Worlds." A good many other men in those South-Eastern counties, where Puritanism was always strong, must have been leading in 1631 a somewhat similar life. Sturdy drovers and graziers of a not uncommon type; but with something stirring within them peculiar to the time. To that special spiritual fermentation the name of "hypochondria" appears to have been given by the neighbours who escaped the infection. Of the hypochondria in Oliver's case all that we hear of the symptoms is that he often thought he was at death's door, sending for Dr Simcott at midnight,—the ailment however being complicated by spleen, and "fancies about the Town Cross." Seeing what was to come of the hypochondria from which Oliver and others suffered, there must have been more in it than "fancies about the Town Cross." An adequate diagnosis of the disease might perhaps help to explain a good deal that is rather inexplicable. Within a few years of this midsummer calm, the strangest, wildest, most subversive, theories of government were to be put in practice; were at least to become the subject of heated discussion in hall and hamlet, in the synod and in the senate. There was a common bond no doubt which gave a certain unity to the discordant voices. The Fifth Monarchy Men, for instance, were only Puritans run mad. The governing idea appears to have been that in some way or other (the *mode* was the occasion of infinite controversy) the temporal power should be made subject to the spiritual. It was (under divers disguises) the old claim of Thomas Cartwright, that the civil magistrate should "lick the dust off the feet of the Church;" of the Scottish General Assemblies, that the "acts and constitutions of the Kirk are of higher authority than those of any earthly King." The State was the *Civitas Dei*. Of a perfectly ordered commonwealth, the King was God. The Presbyterian would have been content had the power to bind and to loose, in this world and the next, been entrusted to the Courts of the Church. The Independent was prepared to go further,—between the individual believer, or the individual congregation, and the God whose counsels they shared, no Court, temporal or ecclesiastical, should come. Cromwell was of this persuasion,—latterly at least,—driven thereto, it may be, by what he had seen of arrogant folly and ineptitude in the ministers of the Kirk.

When such ideas were abroad, it was natural that the men who shared them should believe that there was a close union between the seen and the unseen. The miraculous element in life had not been withdrawn, though its special manifestation depended of course upon the mood of the believer. Even a free-thinking philosopher, like Lord Herbert of Cherbury, looked for confirmation from Heaven before he ventured to publish a philosophical treatise. "Being thus doubtful in my chamber, one fair day in the summer, my casement being open towards the South, the sun shining clear and no wind stirring, I took my book 'De Veritate' in my hand, and kneeling on my knees, devoutly said these words:—'O Thou eternal God, author of the light which now shines upon me, and giver of all inward illuminations, I do beseech Thee, of Thy infinite goodness, to pardon a greater request than a sinner ought to make; I am not satisfied whether I shall publish this book 'De Veritate;' if it be for Thy glory, I beseech Thee give me some sign from Heaven; if not, I shall suppress it.' I had no sooner spoken these words, but a loud though yet gentle noise came from the heavens (for it was like nothing on earth), which did so comfort and cheer me, that I took my petition as granted, and that I had the sign I demanded, whereupon also I resolved to print my book." The author of the 'De Veritate' was a literary man to whom the gift of articulate speech had been given. But what precisely was fermenting in the hearts of the unlettered men around him could not well be guessed. The mood of many was, it may be presumed, more or less morbid. The Apostles wearied while waiting for the return of their Lord. Gloom settled upon the soul of the English Puritan when it appeared that the building of the *Civitas Dei* had been indefinitely delayed. The inward spiritual turmoil, however, was sternly repressed. Like Oliver, they continued to farm and brew. The gloomy apprehensions of coming wrath and judgment did not find voice till later. The sea when agitated by a ground swell may be shaken to its centre; but the wave does not break on the surface. So it may have been during these years of appa-

## CHARLES I.

*Three Heads, painted to assist the sculptor Bernini, to execute a Bust (since lost).*

From the painting by Sir Anthony Vandyke, in the Collection of Her Majesty the Queen at Windsor Castle.

rently unbroken calm. We are assured that, in each class of society, men and women were to be found by whom (as it were the sough of the wind) the breath of the Lord had passed. The chosen vessels might be few as yet,—comparatively few even for years to come, though as the cause prospered the number rapidly increased, as was natural. The note of an intense and high-strung enthusiasm is easily imitated by pretenders, especially when the expression (as too often happened in Cromwell's experience) is grotesque and eccentric. Cromwell for his part worked off a dangerous excess by riotous irony and fervent prayer; how much was genuine, especially towards the end when he was racked by ambition as well as hypochondria, it is hard to say. We may well believe that the language of religious emotion,—the use of Puritanic shibboleths,—was natural at first; as he mounted step by step to an undreamt-of eminence, it became partly habit, partly art. The weapon which had served him so well could not be laid aside, although the mood in which it was first used had passed—not to return. He may have deceived himself at times as he deceived others; he may have striven to repent in dust and ashes, and with sobs and groans audible in the silence of night to those who watched, sought other than priestly absolution; but temporal policy had been his bane; and the dying soldier had ceased to be sustained by the early conviction that he was engaged in a Holy War, and held a Divine Commission.

Of Cromwell I shall have more to say in the sequel. He is to me (in spite of his success, nay because of his success) in some respects a tragic figure. All his life, even when in camp and Court, he was a solitary man. The men he led, the men he lived with, would gladly have stamped out the heresies of High Church doctors and prelates as we stamp out rinderpest. But for Cromwell, the reign of the Saints would have been harsher than it was,—an English Inquisition hardly less severe than the Spanish. He would have liked well to work with other instruments; civil and military servants swayed by irregular and visionary impulses were really not to his taste; but his evil Fate was too strong for him. He had estranged, unwillingly it may have been, all the forces of English society whose co-operation he desired, on which he would fain have rested his rule. He complained bitterly of their hostility, ignorant apparently that he himself had made the gulf impassable. His bodily health must have improved before the Civil War began; but there were discords in his nature which were never healed. He was "possessed" by a great passion which quickened and exalted his faculties into fierce ecstasy and a fever of devotion; yet he had a cool head and a grim humour. He was austere; but he was fervid. A fire burned beneath that plain garb and that uncomely visage. Frost blisters, and every nerve of Cromwell's iron frame thrilled with sensitive life. On one side—immense coolness, profound calculation; on the other—the *hysterica passio* of Lear.

But on the whole, as he lay on his deathbed, he must have felt that his life had been a failure. He had built on the sand, and he knew it. Nor had he built with entire integrity. Clarendon, who did not love him, admits that the Huntingdon brewer or drover acquitted himself on his elevation with perfect tact. Even in the highest place his manner was faultless. "As he grew into place and authority, his parts seemed to be raised, as if he had had concealed faculties, till he had occasion to use them; and when he was to act the part of a great man, he did it without any indecency, notwithstanding the want of custom." But, all the same, his inner nature had deteriorated. He had not adhered to his high ideals. He had put Charles to death because he was a "tyrant" who had shed "the blood of the Saints," but his own rule was ten times more arbitrary and autocratic, a hundred times more unconstitutional. He was to establish, as Milton fondly anticipated, the *Civitas Dei*. A military dictatorship was a poor reflection of the City of God. That is the pathos of it. He had been forced to take the path which he knew was the lower and less noble,—the less excellent way. Possibly he was not altogether to blame: it might be that (whatever the cause) he could only choose the second best.

"Men must endure
His going hence, even as their coming hither:
Ripeness is all."

JOHN MILTON.

From a Miniature by Alexander Cooper, in the South Kensington Museum

Ripeness is all. But Cromwell's work had not ripened, nor had his character. The fields were not yellow unto harvest. He had triumphed over all his enemies, and many of his friends; yet the conviction of defeat must have been always present, and, to a man of his temperament, always galling. The sense of irretrievable loss, of a loss that can never be quite repaired in this world, is, as it seems to me, the supremest tragedy.

Until the early autumn of 1636, the midsummer calm remained unbroken. What discontent there might be did not reach the surface. But undoubtedly, as subsequent events proved, there were not a few ready to take advantage of any indiscretion on the part of the King. For nearly ten years, warned by Wentworth, he had walked warily. But the good time was nearly over. The legality of the levy of ship-money was about to be tested by Hampden; and the use of Laud's prayer-book in St. Giles's was to drive the Scots, ever till then loyal to the Stuarts, into flat rebellion. When the spark once fell, there was no saying how far the conflagration might spread.

LOUIS XIV. AT MARLY.

From the painting by Van der Meulen, in the Collection of Her Majesty the Queen

## CHAPTER SEVEN.

### THE EVE OF THE CONFLICT.

For eleven years—1629-1640—the English Parliament did not meet. It is admitted on all hands that until 1637—when the Scottish troubles broke out—these years were quite exceptionally peaceful and prosperous. It was a period of personal rule; but even the writers who are most averse to personal rule are constrained to allow that the suspension of sittings at Westminster does not appear to have occasioned any acute or wide-spread displeasure. How is the tranquillity to be accounted for? Why did the nation calmly and even cheerfully acquiesce in the prolongation of the parliamentary recess? Why was the peace not broken? These questions merit further consideration.

Mediæval devotion or ambition turned Europe into a huge spiritual camp. The State might then not inaptly have been represented with a sword in one hand and a Bible in the other, like a fighting bishop. The Old and New Testaments formed, in a sense, the statute-law of Christendom. Every citizen was, or ought to be, a soldier in this army. The heretic was a deserter, and desertion was punished with military rigour. The idea of a righteous dissent was unfamiliar and unwelcome. Freedom of belief, liberty of discussion, were incompatible with military discipline. So that a religious test naturally became the test of civil capacity. Unless a man believed in the Apostles' Creed he was not qualified to serve—still less to command. In fact it was difficult to find any place for him in this world; he was untrue to the colours, and should be dealt with accordingly.

In such a State there could be only one Church tolerated by law. It would have been as logical to tolerate treason as to tolerate dissent.

It might have been thought that the Reformation would have favoured liberty. But it was not so. The reformed communities were as intolerant as the unreformed. In the England of 1630, the one Church that had recognised legal existence was the Anglican. The Catholic Chapel was proscribed—so was the Conventicle. Every loyal citizen was bound to attend the services of the Church established by law,—recusants, Popish or Puritan, being liable to punishment. This was Laud's creed; but Laud was not singular; the creed was common to all the Churches. Had the Puritan been in power there would have been a Puritan Church, and a Puritan Church only. No rival communion would have been tolerated by Rome.

In 1630 the sectaries were in a minority. For some time they had apparently been losing ground. Puritanism was not popular at the moment; and the austere rule of the Saints would not have been heartily welcomed by any class of Englishmen. Laud was fussy no doubt, and his passion for ceremonial conformity was excessive; but it was generally recognised that the Church of which Charles was the head would be less oppressive and illiberal than the Church of the Commons. The Commons were insisting on uniformity of belief, whereas Laud would be satisfied with uniformity of ritual. Compared with Eliot or Pym, Laud was a Broad Churchman.

When the indictment against Laud is carefully scrutinised, the unprejudiced inquirer is surprised to find that so many of the charges are frivolous. It must be admitted that he was indiscreet; and once at least the indiscretion was gross, and was followed by fatal disaster. Yet many of the changes which he advocated were harmless, and some of them were distinctly in the right direction. Even of these however it must be said that the majority were ill-advised. They were ill-advised in respect that the effect they were likely to produce upon the public mind had not been sufficiently considered. No statesman can afford to disregard the element of Discontent. If in a distempered state of public feeling, a certain course of action (not intrinsically objectionable) is certain to excite suspicion and distrust, a wise ruler will hold his hand.

Laud restored and purified the great metropolitan Cathedral which had literally been turned into a den of thieves. *That*, popular or unpopular, (and it was unpopular with the faction which held that it was "more agreeable to the rules of piety to demolish such old monuments of superstition and idolatry than to keep them standing") was probably an imperative duty which the Bishop of London was bound to discharge; but not a few of his reforms were unseasonable, were the cause of bitter strife, and might with advantage have been delayed. Laud had, in short, an unhappy habit of rubbing his flock the wrong way. The annoyances that he inflicted upon numbers of prosperous law-abiding citizens, who were perfectly willing to remain good Churchmen if let alone, were trivial no doubt; but the constant buzzing of a fly about one's ears is sometimes more irritating than a serious mishap.

Even during the wonderfully tranquil years of "the tyranny," the ecclesiastical calm had not been quite unbroken. There was an occasional ripple on the water. The Declaration that there should be no wrangling over the mysteries of religion had provoked considerable controversy. The Declaration that after service on Sundays the people might continue to enjoy their holiday in the orthodox old English fashion was gall and wormwood to the austere sectary. The austere sectary was doubly aggrieved. He delighted in theological discussion. The insoluble problems which surround us in this inscrutable universe were, so to speak, his meat and drink. On the other hand the Sabbath, as he called it, was a day of gloom which the sinner should spend on his knees. Heine's wild jest, that a beadle got up on a long ladder and took down the sun, was barely an exaggeration of the Puritanic sentiment about the first day of the week. (The contemporary joke was hardly so good; it was alleged that the men of Banbury, where the sectaries were rampant, hanged their cats on Monday for catching mice on Sunday.) To exhort people who were already prone to mirth to pass the afternoon of "the Lord's day" in idle games was an offence which Heaven would not readily forgive. For those who recommended abstention from serious debate, and participation in carnal sports, a day of reckoning was surely at hand.

Both Declarations are in their way curious—curious and suggestive. The Declaration on uniformity may still be read in the English Prayer-Book; and, offering as it does copious matter for meditation, may have proved serviceable when a prosy discourse by a prosy parson was being unseasonably prolonged. The voice is the voice of Charles; but Laud, it may be presumed, was the author. "Being by God's Ordinance," the King is made to say, "according to Our just Title, Defender of the Faith, and Supreme Governour of the Church, within these Our Dominions, We hold it most agreeable to this Our Kingly Office, and Our own religious Zeal, to conserve and maintain the Church committed to Our Charge in the Unity of true Religion and in the Bond of Peace; and not to suffer unnecessary Disputations, Altercations, or Questions to be raised which may nourish Faction both in the Church and Commonwealth."

On this Preamble, the Declaration proceeds:—"We have therefore upon mature Deliberation, and with the Advice of so many of Our Bishops as might conveniently be called together, thought fit to make this Declaration following:- That for the present, though some differences have been

Group of 5 Miniatures.

.LES I. WHEN A YOUTH (above), PRINCE RUPERT (l. r.), LORD STRAFFORD (after Sir A. Vandyke (centre)), CHARLES LOUIS, Count Palatine, Brother of Prince Rupert (after P. Oliver (right)), MARQUIS OF MONTROSE (after S. Camp... below).

In the Collection of the Duke of Buccleuch, at Montague House, London.

ill raised, yet We take comfort in this that all Clergymen within Our Realm have always most willingly subscribed to the Articles established; which is an Argument to Us that they all agree in the true, usual, literal meaning of the said Articles: and that even in those curious points, in which the present differences lie, men of all sorts take the Articles of the Church of England to be for them: which is an argument again that none of them intend any desertion of the Articles established. That therefore in these both curious and unhappy differences, which have for so many hundred years, in different times and places, exercised the Church of Christ, We will that all further curious search be laid aside, and these disputes shut up in God's promises as they be generally set forth to us in the holy Scriptures and the general meaning of the Articles of the Church of England according to them; and that no man hereafter shall either print, or preach, to draw the Article aside any way, but shall submit to it in the plain and full meaning thereof, and shall not put his own sense or comment to be the meaning of the Article, but shall take it in the literal and grammatical sense."

*Grata quies.* From the dawn of history man had been accustomed to speculate upon his Destiny. How? Whence? Whither? But there was to be no more indulgence of an inconvenient and unsanctified curiosity. All further curious search was to be laid aside. The notion that a primitive and ineradicable instinct of human nature could be erased by a Royal Prohibition was very characteristic of Laud.

But his motives in recommending the issue of the Declaration have, I think, been misunderstood. His contemporaries fancied that his Protestantism was half-hearted. It would have been truer to say that the indiscreet fervour of his Protestant zeal accounts for many of his indiscretions. The Catholic, who boasted that he belonged to an infallible Church, taunted Protestantism with its divisions. Laud, who held that Canterbury was in no way inferior to Rome, may have asked himself, Is it not possible to present an undivided front to the enemy? Why should he be advised that there are divisions in the camp? If we cannot heal the strife, do not at least let us noise our contentions abroad. The religion of Protestants may be defended on the broadest rational grounds; but till the defence is ready (Laud was aiding Chillingworth in the preparation of his great work) controversy among ourselves is suicidal.

There would have been much in such a plea, though the Puritan might not have found it convincing. It is to be apprehended, indeed, that by this time the more extreme section of the sectaries would have retorted that Laud if not a Catholic was an Anglican, and that loyalty to Anglicanism was not loyalty to truth.

The republication in 1633 of the "Declaration of Sports," which had been originally issued in the previous reign, might have passed without observation, had Laud not required that it should be read in churches. He held apparently that the parson was an officer of the State, and bound to read official documents for the information of the people. But the conforming Puritans (that is to say the Puritan clergy within the Church) were naturally indignant. On the other hand the "Sunday Meetings" were still popular with the farmers and labourers in the outlying counties, who if these customary gatherings were taken from them would, it was said, "have no recreations at all to refresh their spirits," except tippling in the public-houses, and talking politics over their ale. So it was declared that as soon as the service was over, "the King's good people" of each parish were "not to be disturbed, letted, or discouraged from any lawful recreation such as dancing, either men or women, archery for men, leaping, vaulting, or any other such harmless recreation, nor from having of May-games, Whit-ales, and Morris dances, and the setting up of May-poles, and other sports therewith used, so as the games be had in due and convenient time, without impediment or neglect of Divine service."

There were others besides the Puritans who held that Sabbath sports and pastimes did not tend to edification. Though many of the clergy approved, the contemporary evidence is rather conflicting. On the whole it rather consists with modern experience. The words of the "Book of Sports" must recall to some of us the pleasant Sundays we have spent in the Bavarian or Austrian Tyrol. *There* the old English fashion of turning the afternoon of the first day of the week into a friendly festival is still observed, and, so far as one can judge, the wholesome and robust life of the mountaineer does not suffer from his Sunday gaiety. The morals of the Irish cottars and crofters are unimpeachable,—contrasting favourably with the morals of their more Puritanic neighbours in England and Scotland—but all over the island, and especially in remote Kerry and Connemara, the Sunday dance on the green outside the chapel—seldom missed by lad or lass—is the great event of the week.

Though it cannot be asserted that at any time of his life Milton would have taken part in a dance on the green, there was yet an element in his nature which had no tincture of Puritanism. It was really against manifestations of this Puritan austerity, that he protested in more than one fine passage of the "Areopagitica." "If we think to regulate printing, thereby to rectify manners, we must regulate all recreations and pastimes, all that is delightful to man. No music must be heard, no song be set or sung, but what is grave and Doric. There must be licensing dancers, that no gesture, motion, or deportment be taught our youth, but what by their allowance shall be thought honest: for such Plato was provided of. It will ask more than the work of twenty licensers to examine all the lutes, the violins, and the guitars in every house; they must not be suffered to prattle as they do, but must be licensed what they may say. And who shall silence all the airs and madrigals that whisper softness in chambers? The windows also, and the balconies, must be thought on; there are shrewd books, with dangerous frontispieces, set to sale: who shall prohibit them, shall twenty licensers? The villages also must have their visitors to inquire what lectures the bagpipe and the rebec reads, even to the ballatry and the gamut of every municipal fiddler; for these are the countryman's Arcadias, and his Montemayors."

There was thus no particular reason why the nation should be anxious that Laud should be removed from the conduct of ecclesiastical affairs. Men like Falkland and Chillingworth and Hales were nearer akin to him than to the intemperate fanatics who would have taken his place; while to men on a lower level than the great latitudinarians, the gloomy asceticism of Puritanism had as yet failed to commend itself as a desirable rule of life.

Nor as yet were the sober majority of Englishmen convinced that the State would be more prosperous or better governed if power was taken from King and Lords, and vested in the Commons. Hitherto it had been a contest between King and Commons; and, on the whole, they were inclined to side with the King. The King's position was in accordance with precedent. The pretensions of the Commons were unprecedented. In the King, not in the Commons, the executive power had been vested by the Constitution. Their experience of recent Parliaments, moreover, had tended to confirm the views of eminent statesmen like Bacon and Cecil. Bacon and Cecil had held that the Commons were not yet capable of governing wisely or well. The more thoughtful constitutionalists could not but agree with them. It seemed to them that, even in its own interest, unlimited authority ought not to be entrusted to a single assembly. An assembly which is a law to itself is constantly tempted to listen to rash and imprudent counsel. Where there is no Court of Appeal to moderate and restrain, a Court of First Instance is not to be trusted;—experience having shown that it will go persistently astray. When a legislative assembly, presuming on its omnipotence, indulges in fads and freaks, in action which must necessarily lead to national disaster, the public confidence is shaken, the patience of the people is exhausted. A single House, so powerful as to be irresponsible, is moreover an anomaly in a system which claims to be representative. Some such reasoning made Falkland a royalist. He saw the Commons becoming more and more violent. The country was already on the brink of the abyss; and the lower House had lost, or was losing, all command of itself.

Whatever the cause of the general content, it is admitted that as late as 1637 or 1638 Charles's fortunes were still unclouded. Mr. Gardiner is pleased to qualify his admissions; but their general purport cannot be mistaken. Here are a few sentences culled at random from his pages.

1630, "Those who still continued to resist payment were no longer assured of the support of their fellow-merchants. Before the year 1630 came to an end a treaty of peace was signed with Spain. Trade revived with the cessation of hostilities, and the mass of persons engaged in commerce were indisposed to hold back from the pursuit of wealth for the sake of a political principle." 1632, "At home all things appeared tame and quiet. English life seems to be unruffled by any breeze of discontent." "One great advantage Charles had. The lawyers began to rally to his side." "It is not strange if many lawyers preferred the silken chains of the Court to the iron yoke of a popular assembly, not yet conscious of the necessity of submitting to those restraints which it was one day to impose upon itself." 1633, "Never in spite of all that had occurred had civil war appeared further off than in the spring of 1633. Never did there seem to be a fairer prospect of overcoming the irritation that had prevailed four years before." 1636, "To all outward appearances Charles's authority had never been stronger than in the summer of 1636." "We sit here," said Secretary Coke," "thankful in true devotion for this wonderful favour towards us; we enjoy peace and plenty; we are like to those who, resting in a calm haven, behold the shipwreck of others wherein we have no part, save only in compassion to help them with our prayers." 1637, "Never to the inexperienced had Charles's affairs appeared in a more prosperous condition. Opposition at home seemed to have been silenced by the declaration of the judges." "In the summer of 1637, more than eight years had passed away since Parliament had met at Westminster. During those years, in spite of threats of war, which Charles had neither the nerve nor the means to carry out, peace had been maintained, and with the maintenance of peace the material prosperity of the country had been largely on the increase." 1638, "Never since the accession of the Stuart dynasty had the finances been in so flourishing a condition as in the spring of 1638. The great customs which had for some years been farmed for £150,000 were let for £165,000." After reading testimony like this (and much more to the same effect might be quoted) one is tempted to say to Mr. Green and his following as Sidney Smith said to his colleagues of the early *Edinburgh Review*,—"Lay aside your Whiggish delusions of ruin; learn to look the prosperity of the country in the face, and bear it as well as you can."

There was of course the initial difficulty of providing a sufficient revenue, but the national prosperity was advancing by leaps and bounds: as late as 1638 there had been no relapse or abatement; and only financial purists were inclined to make the continued collection of tonnage and poundage, and other dues, an occasion for heated invective. The King's government needed to be carried on; and there was probably a general impression that the Commons in withholding the customary supplies had failed to act with perfect fairness to Charles. The people were not going to quarrel with their Sovereign although, in spite of the most frugal living, he might have failed to make both ends meet.

The truce is said to have been broken when Charles resolved to add to the public revenue by the levy of ship-money. It might possibly be more correct to say that the levy occasioned little agitation until Hampden and others declined to pay their share of the assessment. Hampden, after Falkland, is the most gracious and attractive figure that the civil strife produced; but his fame is rested, surely imprudently, on a somewhat narrow basis. For his heroic conduct in resisting payment of a county rate no words of eulogy, it would appear, can be excessive. One does not exactly see where the heroism comes in. Many worthy people have gone into Court about their taxes without attaining immortality. It was by a mere accident indeed that Hampden's case was selected for trial by the Crown. Any fame there was to be gained should rather have accrued to his counsel; and in fact St. John's speech for the defence was luminous and masterly.

The sea-board counties had been bound to aid the Sovereign in the protection of the Narrow Seas by providing a certain number of ships for the navy. Charles intimated that in lieu of the ships he would accept a money payment. Thereafter the payment was extended to the inland counties. It was contended, probably with justice, that the obligation could not be altered or extended except by legislation, and that the exaction even in the maritime counties was of doubtful legality. The majority of the judges, however, took a different view.

Much has been written on the vexed question of ship-money. The question of technical legal right may fairly be left to the judgment of the Court. It is easy to assert that the judges were corrupt, or that they were prejudiced and narrow-minded. The litigant who fails is always apt to lay the blame on the Court. But the judges listened with close attention; there was no attempt to browbeat counsel; and the argument of the majority is not wanting in force. When we leave technicalities, and consider the claim on its merits, it can hardly be denied that Charles's plea was substantially sound. There is no doubt that England needed a navy. The times were out of joint; the great Continental Powers were far from friendly; and without an adequate naval force there might have been national disaster. It was an opponent of the government who wrote: "His Majesty has directed new writs of an old edition to the ports and maritime counties, to maintain a proportion of shipping for the safeguard of the Narrow Seas, according to the law and custom of England, which is very needful, for the French have prepared a fleet, and challenge a dominion in the seas where anciently they durst not fish for gurnets without license." To confine the contribution to the maritime counties was obviously unfair. The navy is a national concern in which all citizens are interested. We are members one of another; we must bear one another's burdens. This was the equitable plea preferred by the King, the Privy Council, and the judges. In the writs themselves the demands were justified on the ground "that as all are concerned in the mutual defence of one another so all might set to their helping hands for the making of such preparations as, by the blessing of God, may secure this realm against the dangers and extremities which have distressed other nations, and are the common effects of war whenever it taketh a people unprepared." And the opinions of the judges were to the same effect.

It was not denied, indeed, that in a case of urgent necessity, of imminent danger to the Commonwealth, the reserved power of the Sovereign might be properly exercised. It cannot be said perhaps, without a touch of exaggeration, that in 1636 the urgency was extreme; but St. John admitted that on the matter of urgency the Sovereign's determination was final; and that no valid distinction could be drawn between the rate-payers in inland and maritime counties. It would have been better, no doubt, had Parliament been consulted. But Charles had good reason to fear that, if Parliament met, no supply whatever would be voted. So far as he could judge from recent experience, considerations affecting the public safety would not weigh with the Commons. The pretensions of the lower House to uncontrolled authority had of late years been perilously pressed. Unless the Sovereign were to become a cypher, these pretensions could not be recognised. Were Parliament summoned, the impending conflict would be precipitated; and anything was better than the prolonged anarchy which such a conflict would probably involve. Charles, in his defence of the prerogative, might be unduly obstinate; but a time must have come when the most pacific ruler could yield no more.

Whatever these arguments may be worth, there is always this to be said for Charles—that the produce of the light burdens that he laid upon his people were used exclusively in their interest. Not a penny was diverted from the public service. The expenditure was national. The tyrant who impoverishes his people that he may live in selfish luxury is a hateful object. But Charles was the most frugal of monarchs. His household expenses were severely limited. It was said that even the palace linen was in rags. Henrietta Maria had to direct that her bedroom shutters should be closed before a foreign visitor was admitted. Were the light obscured, the ragged coverlet might escape observation!

The exaction of ship-money was no doubt unpopular in many of the counties. Ratepayers always grumble when a new rate is imposed; but in the course of a year or two the grievance is forgotten. There is no reason to believe that the agitation caused by the levy of ship-money would have

CHARLES I., QUEEN HENRIETTA MARIA, AND PRINCE HENRY

From the painting by Daniel Mytens, in the Collection of Her Majesty the Queen, at Buckingham Palace

led to revolutionary excess. Unless a Parliament had been summoned the decision of the judges would probably have been accepted as conclusive; and but for the Scottish troubles it is improbable that Parliament would have been summoned until the irritation had died out. To the troubles in Scotland the English revolution was indirectly due; indirectly only, however; for, without combustible material of some kind within England itself, such a sudden flame, such a widespread conflagration, could hardly have risen.

But the Scottish trouble was undoubtedly very serious. For that trouble Charles as King, and Laud as Archbishop, were jointly responsible. It is lamentably true that from the day of the tumult in St. Giles's Church, Charles's course was steadily downward.

Scottish Churchmen, however, have been barely fair either to Charles or his father. Mr. Carlyle appeared to think that the "Tulchan Bishop" was invented by James. The "Tulchan Bishop" was, in fact, invented by Morton; and the milk, I suspect, had ceased to flow before Morton's death. The truth is that both James and Charles had done much to restrain the rapacity of the nobles, and to provide a more adequate living for the ministers. The mistakes they made must have appeared comparatively trivial to men of broad intelligence. They seem to have been ignorant of the importance attached to the Geneva gown and a simple service by zealous Calvinists. They said in effect: We shall see that you are fairly treated by the laity; that the meagre revenues of the Kirk are substantially increased: on the other hand you will not object to adopt certain seemly forms which will tend towards uniformity of worship throughout the kingdom. The plea was reasonable enough; and those who preferred it were no doubt surprised at the hostility which it provoked. The Kirk of Knox had not been without a ritual of a kind; the bald and unimpressive service—nude to indecency—which we are used to associate with Scottish Presbyterianism was of later growth. For *it* the Westminster Puritans are responsible; and it is not impossible that the fierce agitation which Laud's innovations roused may have been due to the fact that Puritanism, suppressed in England, had crossed the Border, and that the more ardent spirits in the Kirk were already ripe for revolt.

But why Charles, when he found not only the Church and the nobles but the people as one man against him, should have persisted in inviting a conflict which, in any view, would strain his scanty resources to the utmost, and which might end (as it did) in irretrievable disaster, has never been explained. Laud no doubt was his adviser, and Laud was notoriously indiscreet; but only madness—the madness with which the gods afflict those who are bound to perish—can altogether account for such prodigious folly.

In 1633 Charles had returned for the first time to the land of his birth. His coronation as King of Scots took place during that year. "Clouds of suspicion touching religion" were already hanging about; and the ecclesiastical ceremonial at Holyrood was not entirely approved. Laud was with the King to perform the service,—"Show them how an Artist could do it," as Mr. Carlyle sarcastically observes. In spite of smouldering animosities Charles was well received; even in their darkest hours, the Stuarts could count on many a loyal Scot. But it was a changed world when his next visit was paid.

It would be difficult to explain precisely to others than Scottish lawyers how James and Charles succeeded in making ampler provision for the ill paid clergy of Scotland. The Church lands had been seized at the Reformation by the "lean and hungry nobles," who were not prepared to resign the revenues, or any share of the revenues, without a struggle. But Charles insisted that the miserable "stipends" must be augmented out of the "teinds," and after an angry conflict the nobles gave way. But they were ill-pleased; their resentment at what they regarded as confiscation was never appeased, and led to divers "tragedies." Since 1633 there has been little change in the law, which fills many tedious pages in the legal manuals. For my present purpose, a brief extract from Erskine's "Institute" will suffice. "Besides the other powers granted to the Commission of Tithes by the Act of 1633 they were authorised to modify reason able stipends to the parochial clergy out of the tithes. By a former commission which had been appointed by Parliament for the same purpose in 1617 the lowest rate of stipend that was to be modified to any minister was 500 merks Scots, or five chalders of victual, unless when the whole fruits of the benefice fell short of that quantity; and the highest was 1,000 merks or ten chalders of victual. By the Act of 1633, cap. 8, the minimum was raised to eight chalders of victual, where victual-rent was paid, or proportionally in money; which proportion is, by a posterior clause in the statute declared to be 800 merks unless where there shall be a reasonable cause for giving less. But neither that nor any subsequent commissions of tithes were limited, as to their powers of altering the old maximum fixed by the act of 1617. And therefore now that the expense of living is so much heightened, the commission-court exercise a discretionary power of augmenting stipends considerably above that maximum where there is enough of free tithes in the parish. The reasons which chiefly move the court to grant augmentations are that the parish is a place of more than ordinary resort, or that the cure is burdensome, or that the necessaries of life give a high price in that part of the country, or that the scanty allowance of stipend in that parish bears too small a proportion to the weight of the charge."

It cannot be said that the clergy were grateful. Rome was still the mystical Babylon, and the rumour that a "popish" prayer-book was in preparation had been assiduously circulated and widely credited. Some of the "ceremonies" that James had introduced, such as kneeling at Communion, were viewed with disrelish. The nobles were jealous of the bishops, who, indeed, were nowhere popular. In these circumstances it was clear that a Crusade against episcopal government might be readily organised. A cause in which the great nobles, the parochial clergy, and the commonalty, were united could hardly fail to win. From the days of Knox, "the Congregation of Jesus Christ" had been fiercely fanatical; Scotland was not a school where toleration was taught; and any spark would serve to light the flame of revolt.

Charles was crowned in 1633; but it was not till July, 1637, that the "popish" prayer-book was introduced at St. Giles's. Jenny Geddes has been relegated to the region of myth; but there can be no doubt that within and without the Church an angry riot took place; that dangerous missiles were thrown at surpliced dignitaries; and that the offence of "saying Mass at one's lug" was followed by swift retribution. Had Charles been well advised, a place of repentance might even then have been found. But his pride was wounded, and the opportunity was allowed to pass. James or Charles might threaten the "stubborn Kirk;" but, do what they might, it would not "stoop more to the English pattern." The agitation went on, gathering in force and volume, until it culminated in Glasgow Assemblies, Solemn Covenants, and the Lowlands in arms.

The Solemn League and Covenant signed in the Greyfriars churchyard, under the shadow of the Castle rock, has supplied the text for many a picturesque discourse. That there were many honest Covenanters need not be doubted. That they were profoundly intolerant goes without saying. Whoever "came not to the help of the Lord against the mighty," was thundered against, as hopelessly malignant, from Calvinistic pulpits. Under pain of excommunication, every man and woman in the Lowland counties was required to sign the Covenant; and ministers who refused to sign were silenced, maltreated, and driven from their manses. The liberal Aberdeen divines, indeed, until they were forcibly ejected, stood resolutely aloof. "The danger which they foresaw was that which is inseparable from every popular excitement, and especially from every popular religious excitement. They feared for their quiet studies, for their right to draw unmolested their own conclusions from the data before them. They were Royalists; not as Laud and Wren were Royalists, but after the fashion of Chillingworth and Hales. Under the name of authority they upheld the noble banner of intellectual freedom. Under Charles they had such liberty as they needed; under the Covenant they were not likely to have any liberty at all."

LOUIS XIV

From a miniature in the South Kensington Museum

But not a few signed the Covenant who were not honest: whose motives, on the contrary, were base and mercenary. Many of the nobles, at least, were Covenanters, not for the protection of religion but for the protection of their estates. Unless the nation was roused to revolt there might be, they fancied, further "confiscation." So they buckled on their armour, called out their retainers, and, *For Christ's Crown and Covenant* embroidered on their flags, enlisted under Lesley. Hardly seventy years had passed since those of their order who had been concerned in the murder of Darnley had flaunted a banner in the face of Heaven, on which the murdered prince was represented in pathetic appeal: *Judge and avenge my cause, O Lord.* Hypocrisy, however it masquerades, is never lovely; and but for the greedy and unscrupulous nobles of Scotland the Covenant would have left a purer record.

## CHAPTER EIGHT.

### THE POLITICAL CONFLICT.

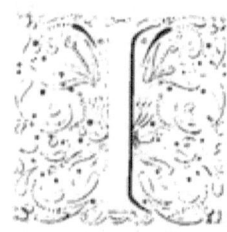

It may be admitted that it is necessary sometimes to look above and beyond the mere letter of the law. When an impracticable Parliament, for instance, refuses to vote any adequate sum for national defence, the King may be entitled to have recourse to those exceptional powers which have been reserved to him by the Constitution, and which under any form of government must be exercised by the executive. But it is a dangerous path to tread; and the ruler who takes it must be prepared (if he has misjudged the forces on either side) for political conflict or civil war.

Unless the Scottish trouble could be composed, it was now plain that the political conflict in England would rapidly become acute.

The Scottish trouble, however, was not easily composed. There had never been much love lost between the turbulent nobles of Scotland and the Stuarts; and now religion had come to add a new complication. The authority of the Crown had been virtually disowned; government at Edinburgh was being carried on provisionally by informal Committees of the Estates; and a large military force drawn mainly from the Lowland counties, and officered by men who, like Dugald Dalgetty, had been in the wars of Gustavus Adolphus, was ready at any moment to cross the Border, and try conclusions with the "Auld enemy." Charles, with his raw and dispirited levies, could make no head against an army of twenty or thirty thousand men, whose discipline was strict, and whose zeal for "Christ's Crown and Covenant" had been fanned by unscrupulous appeal into feverish activity. Twice he was worsted—the first "Bishop's War" was in 1639, the second in 1640; and of both wars the consequences were disheartening, if not disastrous. This angry crowd of fanatical Calvinists, lying like a thunder cloud across the Northern counties, was an emphatic menace. While it emphasized the weakness of Charles's position, it added strength, directly and indirectly, to the position of the disaffected in England. Had he won, had he returned from Scotland in a blaze of triumph, he might have faced Pym and the Parliament with a good courage. But he had failed to win; it might be said indeed that he had been badly beaten: for the Treaty of Ripon had discredited and discouraged the Royalists, and was in fact a certificate of defeat. By that treaty, until its provisions were executed, the two Northern counties were to remain in possession of the Scots army, whose disinterested services were meantime recompensed at the rate of twenty-five thousand pounds a month. A Scots war of religion was seldom conducted at a loss. On this occasion, the English Commissioners were consoled by the assurance that "it is more blessed to give than to receive."

The Royal cause in Scotland was not perhaps so hopeless as it seemed to be when the Treaty of Ripon was signed. North of the Tay the clans were loyal; and should a capable leader hereafter appear the disaster

LETTER OF CHARLES I. TO THE DUKE OF BUCKINGHAM

Fac-simile of the original in the British Museum.

Since [illegible] you [illegible] letters to my Sister & Brother [illegible] I think the [illegible] is the [illegible] as for newes I can say nothing [illegible] Ireland [illegible] the [illegible] have [illegible] upon [illegible] a [illegible] [illegible] have not yet [illegible] it; for [illegible] he has yet not made his formall demands concerning the Ships, to which he has a dilatorie answer, while we heare from France concerning the restitution of our Ships. This is all I have to say to thee at this tyme but that [illegible] that I am [illegible] would be

Your faithfull loving constant friend
Charles R.

might be repaired. The Covenanters had already discovered that the young Montrose was "very sair to be guided;" James Graham had little in common with the zealots who were eager to precipitate a fratricidal war: and it was not impossible that their impolitic violence might drive him sooner or later into the camp of the enemy. Even in the Lowlands there was a latent force of Royalism which would make itself felt when the more moderate Churchmen, who had been persuaded to sign the Covenant, began to realise the gravity of the issues that were involved in the conflict.

But (whatever of good or evil fortune the future might have in store for Scotland) it had become imperatively necessary to summon an English Parliament. Charles's finances were exhausted. Strafford was convinced that further delay would be ruinous, and Strafford was now Charles's most trusted adviser. The "Short Parliament" met on April 13th, 1640. Its career was brief and troubled. It was dissolved on May 5th.

It is still doubtful how far Charles was responsible for its dissolution. Compared with the preceding and succeeding Parliaments, it might be regarded as well affected to the King. It contained a large and influential body of Royalists. There would have been considerable friction, no doubt; it could hardly have approved the war with Scotland; but its mood was not bitterly implacable; and by address and management, by patience and forbearance, the preliminaries of a permanent peace might have been settled. Whoever was responsible for the dissolution of a comparatively friendly assembly incurred a heavy responsibility.

The burden of blame, according to Clarendon, falls on Sir Harry Vane. The elder Vane was the Secretary of State; but he was hardly loyal to the King, his master. Wentworth, who at Charles's request had come over from Ireland, was urgent that a Parliament should be called, and his advice had been reluctantly accepted by the King and his Council. Vane, who was jealous of Wentworth, (now Earl of Strafford) was the friend of Pym and the parliamentary leaders; and he did what he could to stir up strife, and to make concord impossible. Charles had been averse to taking less than twelve subsidies in exchange for the abandonment of ship-money; but after hearing Strafford's earnest plea for moderation, he had instructed Vane to inform the Commons that he would be satisfied with eight. Vane went down to the House, and assured the members that if the supply were not in "the proportion and manner" proposed by the King, it would not be accepted by him. He then, with the Solicitor-General St. John, returned to Whitehall, and reported so unfavourably of the humour and temper of the House, that they induced the King to believe that a hostile motion would be moved and carried. Hence the precipitate dissolution. This is Clarendon's version of the incident. Clarendon was a member of the House and took a leading part in the discussion; but his narrative is, so far, discredited by Mr. Gardiner; and, though I incline to accept it as accurate in the main, it is no doubt open to observation. However this may be, it is admitted that throughout the negotiations, Wentworth was in favour of a conciliatory policy; and there is reason to believe that he bitterly regretted the rupture, and held that the dissolution was mischievous and ill-advised.

But Wentworth was not a man whose loyalty was skin deep. To him more than to most men the poet's lines applied:—

"For loyalty is still the same
Whether it win or lose the game;
True as the dial to the sun,
Although it be not shin'd upon."

He had come from Ireland sorely against his inclination, leaving the fair edifice of law and order, that his strong and resolute will had raised, to crumble within a few months into utter ruin. He had come to help the King through his English and Scottish troubles; and, though his own scheme of accommodation had been wrecked by temper or treachery he did his best to heal the breach. Charles's means were exhausted; Strafford headed a voluntary contribution with £20,000; but the maintenance of a large force, however raw and undisciplined, is costly; and ere long it was found that another Parliament must be summoned. The public mind had been agitated by the ill success of the Scottish wars; the writs were issued amid a storm of angry invective; and the fears of those who held that the new Parliament would be less compliant than the old were more than justified. It was on November 3rd, 1640, that the "Long Parliament" commenced its sittings.

The dissolution of the Short Parliament was fertile of evil to King and people. To it the Iliad of woes that followed may be directly traced. In view of its momentous consequences, it is fair that the reader should have the words of an eye-witness before him. This is Clarendon's narrative—he was then Edward Hyde:—"Both Sir Henry Vane, and the Solicitor-General (whose opinion was of more weight with the King than the others) had made a worse representation of the humour and affection of the House than it deserved, and undertook to know, that if they came together again, they would pass such a Vote against Ship-money, as would blast that Revenue and other branches of the Receipt; which Others believed they would not have had the confidence to have Attempted; and very Few, that they would have had the credit to have Compassed. What followed in the next Parliament, within less than a Year, made it believed, that Sir Henry Vane acted that part Maliciously, and to bring all into Confusion; he being known to have an implacable hatred against the Earl of Strafford, Lieutenant of Ireland, whose destruction was then upon the Anvil. But what transported the Solicitor, who had none of the ends of the other, could not be imagined, except it was his pride and peevishness, when he found that he was like to be of less Authority there, than he looked to be; and yet he was heard with great attention, though his Parts were most prevalent in puzzling and perplexing that discourse he meant to cross. Let their Motives be what they would, they Two and they only, wrought so far with the King, that, without so much Deliberation as the affair was worthy of, His Majesty the next morning, which was on the Fifth of May, near a month after their first meeting, sent for the Speaker to attend him, and took care that he should go directly to the House of Peers, upon some apprehension that if he had gone to the House of Commons, that House would have entered upon some ingrateful discourse; which they were not inclined to do: and then sending for that House to attend him, the Keeper, by His Majesty's Command, Dissolved the Parliament.

"There could not a greater damp have seized upon the Spirits of the whole Nation, than this Dissolution caused; and men had much of the Misery in view, which shortly after fell out. It could never be hoped that more sober and dispassionate men would ever meet together in that place, or fewer who brought ill purposes with them: nor could any man imagine what Offence they had given, which put the King upon that resolution. But it was observed, that in the countenances of Those who had most opposed all that was desired by His Majesty, there was a marvellous Serenity; nor could they conceal the Joy of their hearts: for they knew enough of what was to come, to conclude that the King would be shortly compelled to call another Parliament; and they were as sure, that so many so unbiassed men, would never be elected again.

"Within an hour after the Dissolving, Mr. Hyde met Mr. St. John, who had naturally a great cloud in his Face, and very seldom was known to smile, but Then had a most cheerful aspect, and seeing the other melancholic, as in truth he was from his heart, asked him: 'What troubled him?' who answered: 'That the same that troubled him, he believed troubled most Good men; that in such a time of Confusion, so wise a Parliament, which alone could have found Remedy for it, was so unseasonably dismissed,' the other answered with a little warmth: 'That all was well; and that it must be Worse, before it could be Better; and that this Parliament could never have done what was necessary to be done;' as indeed it would not, what He and His friends thought necessary.

"The King, when he had better reflected upon what was like to fall out, and was better informed of the temper and duty of the House of Commons, and that they had voted a Supply, if Sir Henry Vane had not hindered it by so positive a declaration that His Majesty would refuse it, was heartily Sorry for what he had done; declared with great anger, 'That he had never given him such Authority; and that he knew well that the giving him any Supply would have been welcome to him, because the reputation of his Subjects assisting him in that conjuncture was all that he looked for and considered!'"

Before the Long Parliament began its sittings the more astute leaders on either side must have been calculating the chances of the coming conflict. The issue was extremely uncertain—any confident forecast being out of the question; so long as the conflict remained political the Commons occupied the more commanding position; but should it come to civil war it was probable that the majority of the nation—all those indeed who did not belong to the political class—would rally round the King. That the people as a whole were profoundly conservative does not admit of doubt.

Two forces, whose opposition was vital, were already virtually in the field,—the Royalists, who were mainly Episcopalians, the Parliament men who were largely recruited from the Presbyterians. A third party, composed of moderates, included men like Falkland, Chillingworth, and Hales. In the meantime, alarmed by what they considered an oppressive exercise of the prerogative, the "latitudinarians" inclined to the Parliament; but its political intemperance and its religious intolerance were profoundly distasteful to them; and it was morally certain that sooner or later they would be driven to desert their uncongenial allies and to join the Royalists. These were what might be called the purely English parties; but there were others—of foreign growth or importation—whose principles of action were to some extent incalculable.

With the goodly prospect of civil and religious strife before them, the sterner sectaries, who had gone to the Continent or to America, were flocking home. Democratic in their political principles, it was improbable that they would side with the King; on the other hand, an inquisitorial House of Commons, with a fondness for Presbyterian methods, was even more obnoxious to Independents than Monarchy itself. They did not all come from abroad; they had left friends and relatives behind them, among whom during the intervening years the infection had slowly spread; while among the Puritans of the Eastern counties they found zealous allies. Then there was the Scottish army, permanently encamped, as it seemed, in Durham and Northumberland, and perfectly willing to remain while supplies were plentiful and pay remunerative. The Scots in the meantime favoured the Parliament; but there could be no real union, they frankly declared, until the English, persuaded that presbytery was of divine origin, had turned their bishops adrift, and proscribed the exercise of prelatic worship. The Scots were still, moreover, in spite of surplice and prayer-book, attached to their native Princes; and any proposal to treat a Stuart King with scriptural severity would be keenly resented by the whole nation.

The sympathies of the modern world are with Falkland and his friends. They were reluctant to take any part in a conflict between a King whom they distrusted, and a Parliament which had embarked recklessly, as they held, on a policy of adventure. "On one side Scribes and Pharisees," said Chillingworth, "on the other Publicans and Sinners." The Commons represented the Scribes and Pharisees; and an alliance with the Commons would be actively mischievous. The more ardent spirits among them would take the lead; and where would they stop? They might be willing to use the drag; but when once fairly started, where was any adequate resistance to come from? *Facilis descensus Averni.* Revolutionary pressure would bring about the total collapse and ruin of the State; whereas, even if Charles were worse than he was painted, there were official ties, hereditary traditions, constitutional limitations, which he could not wholly disregard.

The latitudinarians were probably well advised; they were the appointed guardians of the spiritual and intellectual liberty that was in peril; yet it may be said with confidence that, when the Long Parliament met, no man in England had clearly divined by whose hand the blow at liberty would be struck. No one at least could dream that in the Independents, even when drilled and organized by a competent captain, there was the making of an irresistible force.

Upon the whole it may be said that the chances at starting were pretty evenly balanced—though the better fighting men were with the King. The Commons forthwith set themselves to redress the balance.

Within eight days of their meeting, Strafford was impeached. Were Strafford gone, the King's first line of defence would be broken. They were not mistaken,—though they erred in holding that Strafford's aims were inconsistent with the existence of a representative assembly.

I do not feel sure that Wentworth's views on government have been anywhere defined with perfect precision. It is quite possible that no exact definition had occurred to himself, and that he would have found difficulty in stating them categorically. He favoured Parliaments; and he favoured personal rule. These propositions may appear to be mutually destructive. But if we accept Montesquieu's theory of the absolute division of the executive from the legislative authority, so that each power is independent of the other, the main difficulty disappears. It then becomes a question of personal rule against the rule of a collective body. The rooted distrust of representative bodies when they exceed their proper function of initiating and promoting legislation is not confined to men like Bacon, Cecil, or Wentworth. That the tendency of the American democracy at the present moment, for instance, is towards a kind of "one man rule" has been very confidently asserted. The ruler no doubt is to be elected; but once elected the whole executive authority is handed over to him, and he becomes while in office almost as absolute as Czar or Kaiser. "Select the best man, put him in office, give him a free hand, and you will secure better government than if the executive authority were vested in and exercised by a representative assembly. The representative assembly cannot be dispensed with; it is in the public interest that certain public functions should be discharged by a body of men representing the people, as it is in the public interest that certain other functions should be discharged by a single individual. In the Seventeenth Century the ruler was the hereditary Sovereign; in the Nineteenth he is an elected magistrate; but there is no difference in principle." *That* substantially is the argument, and it is not without force; even among ourselves there are not a few who hold that the authority of the Lower House is on the wane; that the Cabinet is superseding the Commons; and that the Prime Minister (when a dominating personality) is superseding the Cabinet. English government is daily becoming more and more a "one man rule."

Strafford's trial is an incident which the apologist of royalty, no less than the parliamentary apologist, would willingly forget. It was one of those high-handed acts of a popular assembly which are not readily forgiven. But the guilt is shared by others. Strafford's execution is the blot on Charles's escutcheon. The King never forgave himself. The bitterness of the surrender hurt him to the end. He held indeed that his own sentence was not altogether unjust, seeing that he had consented to Strafford's death.

Wentworth's main work had been done in Ireland; and what he had been to Ireland is best told in his own words. An admirable summary of his famous defence,—the defence of his Irish government which he submitted to the Privy Council, has been given by Mr. Gardiner; and of it I gladly avail myself:- "Wentworth's defence was a splendid narrative of triumphs achieved. The Church, he said, was relieved from its poverty, and united in doctrine and discipline with the Church of England. The Irish exchequer had been saved from ruin. When he landed there was a yearly deficit of £24,000, and an enormous debt. In a few months the debt would be paid, whilst a sum of £40,000 had been set aside to buy up sources of revenue which had been mortgaged, and which, when recovered, would bring in £9,450 a year. There was an increase of £18,000 in the revenue, and thus as soon as the mortgages were paid off the deficit would be converted into a surplus. Other sources of income might easily be opened, and a considerable saving in the expenditure effected. There would soon be a surplus of £60,000.

"Such an exposition of financial success offered a sore temptation to the hungry English courtiers. Wentworth pleaded earnestly with the Council to support him in his efforts to save the money for the public service.

"He then proceeded to show that he had not sacrificed the interests of the State to those of the Treasury. The soldiers, he said, were well paid and well disciplined. Every man who served in the army had passed in review under his own eyes. When the troops were on the march they

CHARLES I. ON HORSEBACK, WITH GENTLEMAN-ATTENDANT

From the painting in the Collection of Her Majesty the Queen, at Windsor.

paid fairly for everything they took, no longer satisfying their wants by force, as if they had been in an enemy's country. They were now welcome in every place, where before they were an abomination to the inhabitants. The King was well served at the same time. Never had an army been so completely master of Ireland.

"A full treasury and a strong military force may easily be compatible with the direst misgovernment. Wentworth insisted that he was not liable to this reproach. Justice was dispensed to all without acceptance of persons; 'that the poor knew where to seek and to have his relief without being afraid to appeal to his Majesty's catholic justice against the greatest subject;' that 'the great men' were 'contented with reason, because they knew not how to help themselves, or fill their greedy appetites, where otherwise they were as sharp set upon their own wills as any people in the world.' The Commission of defective titles was doing its work, and now that men could call their lands their own without fear of question they were able to devote themselves to the improvement of their estates. The acts of the last Parliament were a boon to the whole people, and 'there was a general and steadfast belief on that side in the uprightness of his Majesty's justice, the people were satisfied, his Majesty by them honoured and blessed, in contemplation of the great and princely benefits and graces they participate of, through his Majesty's wisdom and goodness.'

"Trade flourished no less than agriculture. Two years before pirates had swarmed in the Irish seas. Now the coasts were guarded, and the pirates were no longer heard of. Commerce was rapidly on the increase. Manufactures had been encouraged. The best flax seed had been imported from Holland. Workmen had been brought over from France and the Netherlands. Six or seven looms were already set up, and the foundation of a great industry in the future had been surely laid.

"Wentworth at last turned to the subject which was in the minds of all his hearers. It had been said that in his treatment of offenders he 'was a severe and an austere hard-conditioned man; rather, indeed, a Basha of Buda than the minister of a pious and Christian king.' He carnestly declared that it was not so, that in private life no one could charge him with harshness, and that it was 'the necessity of his Majesty's service' which had forced him to act as he had done."

After such a record of unbroken success, one inclines to agree with Mr. Gardiner that even if Wentworth be taken at his worst, it is hardly possible to doubt that Ireland would have been better off if his sway had been prolonged for twenty years longer than it was. Constitutional pedantry may be carried to mischievous extremes; and after a flood of political commonplace, the vigorous extravagances of Samuel Johnson are sometimes welcome. "Sir," said the lexicographer, "I would not give half a guinea to live under one form of government rather than another." He meant, I presume, that he agreed with Pope :—

"For forms of government let fools contest,
Whate'er is best administered is best."

It was obvious from the day it met that the temper of this Parliament was very different from that of the last. To use a phrase then current it was "a root-and-branch" Parliament. Moreover it was Pym's Parliament,—Pym, a relentless enemy as well as an adroit tactician. Hampden's name is usually associated with Pym's; but as matter of fact Hampden seldom took any conspicuous part in debate, and it must have been his high character rather than his intellectual resources that impressed the House. Pym was the real leader; and Pym had an old score to settle with Strafford. Wentworth had been allied with the popular party when the contest with Buckingham was in progress; and Pym, who had failed to understand that Wentworth cared mainly for good government, and regarded the form with comparative indifference, had been furious with his old friend when he found that he had gone over to the Court. The story runs that before Wentworth left London for York in 1628, he chanced to fall in with Pym. "You are going to leave us, I see," said Pym, "but we will never leave you while your head is on your shoulders."

It was almost inevitable that a House led by Pym and which was bent on making Strafford's motto—"Thorough!"—its own, should fall foul of the haughty and imperious Yorkshireman. While knocking to pieces the whole political and ecclesiastical edifice that Charles and his predecessors had raised, it devoted itself with the keenest zest to the impeachment of the Royalist leaders. Strafford and Laud were both sent to the Tower.

Strafford had been in wretched health for many months. Disease had wasted his powerful frame, and in this crisis of Charles's fortunes he was helplessly crippled. His masterful temper had made him many enemies. —English, Scottish, Irish;—even the courtiers at Whitehall did not relish his simple directness, and his unswerving devotion to public duty. Lucy, Lady Carlisle, appears to have been almost his only confidant at Court, and curiously enough, the reigning beauty was also the friend of Pym. Lady Carlisle was no doubt proud to be the ally of both; and though her political ideas may have been crude, she was obviously of considerable social force and of great attractiveness. Whether she played a part, whether she made a dishonest use of her confidential relations with the Queen, may be matter of controversy: but she was bright and winning, and her charm has been extolled by more than one poet.

Strafford was unwilling to come to town. He was Lord Lieutenant of Ireland, and in Ireland, with the Irish army at his back, he would be safe. He was living at his pleasant home on the Yorkshire moorland; and so long as he remained among his own people Pym was powerless. But he felt instinctively that in the immediate neighbourhood of merciless foes and hostile assemblies his life would be in peril. Charles however was eager to have his most trusted counsellor at his side; and he positively assured the Earl that, if he came, not a hair of his head should be touched. Relying on what he held to be a most solemn engagement, the stricken man went up to Westminster. He would be loyal to the last:—as he had said long before, he would not spare his life for his King.

The Parliamentary leaders may have been spurred into unbecoming activity by apprehensions for their own safety. They were going to accuse Strafford of treason; in their confidential communications with the Scottish insurgents they had committed the crime with which they charged him

There is a Scottish proverb to the effect that it is well to have the "first word of flyting;" and Pym wisely determined to take the initiative. He and his colleagues (unprepared as yet with any evidence) went straight to the Lords and impeached the Lord Lieutenant of Ireland of high treason. Strafford with his hands free might do them an evil turn; Strafford in the Tower would be helpless.

In these last months of his life Strafford behaved very simply and very nobly,—with no undue arrogance, with no undue humility. He had looked for justice, and he hardly expected to die. The word of a King had been given that he should not suffer in his person, honour, or fortune. The charges against him were comparatively frivolous, the most hostile assembly, he thought, could not extract high treason from a policy which had been approved by the Sovereign, and which in the public interest had been eminently successful.

But as the trial proceeded, it became more and more obvious that his enemies were implacable and unscrupulous and that every art of intimidation would be employed to secure a hostile verdict. Both King and Queen in their anxiety to save a devoted servant acted with doubtful prudence. A lying spirit was abroad. Every evil rumour was accepted with avidity. A panic of Irish armies and Popish plots was skilfully fomented. The turbulent London mob was in its ugliest mood. So long as the Lords were required to act as judges they acted with conspicuous fairness. But when the Commons, finding that for lack of evidence impeachment must fail, resorted to an Act of Attainder, they lost heart, and by a small majority gave reluctant consent. It was a harder matter to wring consent from Charles; but he could find no door of escape; bishops and judges plied him with legal and doctrinal casuistry; and in an agony of doubt and bewilderment the fatal words were spoken.

Strafford had left Wentworth, his place in Yorkshire, on the 6th of November, and he arrived in London on the evening of the 9th. He knew that there was a severe struggle before him, and that he must brace himself for the conflict. "I am to-morrow to London," he wrote, "with more dangers beset, I believe, than ever any man went with out of Yorkshire: yet my heart is good and I find nothing cold in me. It is not to be believed how great the malice is, and how intent they are about it. Little less care there is taken to ruin me than to save their own souls." Before he reached London "grievances" were being keenly debated by the Commons. Their name was Legion. The judges, it was declared with epigrammatic bitterness, had overthrown the law and the bishops the gospels. By the 11th, certain Articles of Impeachment had been laid by Pym and his colleagues before the Lords. They were generally to the effect that in England as in Ireland "Thomas, Earl of Strafford, had traitorously endeavoured to subvert the fundamental laws and government of the realm, and instead thereof to introduce an arbitrary and tyrannical government against law, which he had declared by traitorous words, counsels and actions, and by giving His Majesty advice by force of arms to compel his loyal subjects to submit thereto." There were grosser charges—public moneys had been appropriated by him for his own use, and so forth—which no one believed and which it is unnecessary to repeat. Pym's acrimony was so manifest that Strafford was justified in believing that no court—least of all a court of independent Peers—would listen to his partial pleading. He wrote hopefully to his wife:

"As to myself albeit all be done against me that art and malice can devise, yet I am in great inward quietness, and a strong belief God will deliver me out of all these troubles. The more I look into my case the more hope I have, and sure if there is any honour and justice left, my life will not be in danger; and for anything else, time I trust, will salve any hurt which can be done me. Therefore hold up your heart, look to the children and your house, let me have your prayers, and at last by God's good pleasure we shall have our deliverance when we may as little look for it as we did for this blow of misfortune which I trust will make us better to God and man."

The revised indictment was not ready till the end of January. Then two or three weeks elapsed before Strafford's answers were prepared, and the impatient Commons became clamorous at the delay. Their anxiety to see the fallen statesman was extreme. One morning it was rumoured that the Earl was in the barge then passing the House: business was interrupted; and the members flocked to door and window. On the 24th of February Strafford's answers were read to the Lords; but it was not till the 22nd of March that the actual trial began. Pym took the lead,—starting with Irish misgovernment. Of the true condition of Ireland he knew nothing—its chronic misery and anarchy; nor of the vast reformation that Strafford's rule had worked; but inasmuch as Strafford had not adhered closely enough to certain constitutional forms, Strafford, he argued, had been guilty of treason. The only evidence of any value that was adduced were notes of a discussion in the Privy Council which the elder Vane had made,—not the original notes, but copies surreptitiously taken by his son. Vane was Strafford's bitter enemy, and as no Lord of the Council other than Vane had heard the words, it is a fair presumption that they were never uttered. Two witnesses were required to support a charge of treason; and it was gravely argued that Vane was one witness, and his notes or rather the copies of his notes, another! Strafford's answer was conclusive. He denied that he had used the words; but, if he had, they were used in the privacy of the Council Chamber; and if its secrecy was to be invaded he did not think that "any wise or noble person" would hereafter venture to become a Councillor of the King. Nor indeed when fairly weighed did the words convey any treasonable design. "In case of absolute necessity, and upon a foreign invasion of an enemy, when the enemy is either actually entered, or ready to enter, and when all other ordinary means fail, in this case there is a trust left by Almighty God in the King to employ the best and uttermost of his means for the preserving of himself and his people which, under favour, he cannot take away from himself."

In spite of his feeble health, and the strain of acrimonious discussions often protracted from morning till night, Strafford triumphantly asserted his innate superiority. Pym spoke closely from notes,—which occasionally, we are told, went astray, and then the orator faltered and stammered; Strafford used neither note nor memorandum, but spoke right out with natural ease and felicity, and a force of logic that carried instant conviction. It was not till April 13th, that his great speech was made. The Lords were his judges, he said, and to them he would confidently appeal. If every syllable of the most familiar discourse were to be used hereafter as evidence in a criminal cause, "it will be a silent world, and a city will become a hermitage." Where was the statute or common law that had declared the endeavouring to subvert the fundamental laws to be high treason? "We find that in the primitive time, on the sound and plain doctrine of the blessed apostles, men brought in their books of curious art and burnt them. My Lords, it will be likewise, as I humbly conceive, wisdom and providence in your Lordships to cast from you into the fire these bloody and mysterious volumes of constructive and arbitrary measures, and betake yourselves to the plain letter of the Statute that tells you where the crime is, so that you may avoid it. And let us not, my Lords, be ambitious to be more learned in those killing arts than our forefathers were before us." A speech worthy of a great logician closed with a passage worthy of a great orator:—"My Lords, I have now troubled your Lordships a great deal longer than I should have done. Were it not for the interest of the pledges, that a saint in Heaven left me, I should be loth, my Lords.... (here he paused for a moment overcome by his emotion, and then leaving the sentence unfinished continued).... What I forfeit for myself, it is nothing. But I confess that what I forfeit for them, it wounds me very deeply. You will be pleased to pardon my infirmity; something I should have said, but I see I shall not be able, and therefore I will leave it. And now, my Lords, I thank God, I have been by his good blessing towards me taught that the afflictions of the present life are not to be compared to that eternal weight of glory that shall be revealed hereafter. And so, my Lords, even so, with all humility and with tranquillity of mind, I do submit clearly and freely unto your judgment, whether that righteous judgment shall be to life or death, *Te Deum laudamus, te Dominum confitemur*."

The end was near. Strafford had made his peace with the world He had been anxious to say farewell to the venerable primate who was lodged close by, but permission was refused by the Lieutenant of the Tower. He might however petition the Commons. "No," said Strafford, "I have gotten my dispatch from them and will trouble them no more. I am now petitioning a higher court, where neither partiality can be expected nor error feared." Laud however had been informed of Strafford's desire; and from the window of his cell, as the melancholy procession went by to Tower Hill in the early morning, the aged prelate lifted up his hands and blessed his friend. On the scaffold Strafford sent a few last words of greeting to wife and child. "I thank God," he added, as he took off his upper garment, "I am not afraid of death nor daunted with any discouragement rising from my fears, but do as cheerfully put off my doublet at this time as ever I did when I went to bed." The executioner would have covered his eyes. "Thou shalt not bind my eyes," said Strafford, "for I shall see it done." The blow fell, and the wasted body and wearied spirit were at rest,—if it be rest that rounds this little life.

Strafford was executed on May 12th, 1641; Charles's standard was raised at Nottingham on August 22nd, 1642. During these fifteen months the political conflict between King Charles and "King Pym" was carried on with ever growing acrimony. By the summer of 1642 the tension had become so acute that it was probably a relief to all public men, except the small band of Moderates led by Falkland, when Civil War was at length formally declared. There could now, it was too clear, be no real peace until blood had been spilt. Whether the exasperation was due to the action of the King, or to the action of the Commons, it is hard to say; possibly to both; but that the time had come when the quarrel must be settled, not by argument in the Senate House, but by cold steel on the field of battle, could no longer be doubted.

Within a few weeks of Strafford's death Charles had satisfied himself that the aim of Pym and the Parliament was to deprive him of the rights which law and usage had vested in the King of England. On the other hand Pym insisted that whatever was done by the Parliament was done in self-defence. Charles was a despotic ruler, who was engaged in a dangerous conspiracy against true religion and the ancient liberties of Englishmen. The times were out of joint, and men's minds were jaundiced; yet it is hard to believe that Pym was serious. His new version of the old fable—the old fable of wolf and lamb—reads like a burlesque.

It is hardly to be denied that Pym himself was *straining the Constitution*. He was bent on securing the supremacy of the House of Commons. The object may have been laudable; that is matter of opinion; I am dealing with matter of fact. But if Pym had his way the Constitution would unquestionably be cast into the melting pot; when it reappeared (if it reappeared at all) it might be vastly improved, but it would be an altogether different article. The King, and those who stood by him, were entitled to say that they saw no sufficient reason for so iconoclastic an experiment.

The Commons started with a bill which provided that without their own consent they could not be dissolved. But for an accident, the Long Parliament might be still sitting! The bill went to Charles along with the Strafford Bill of Attainder. He failed to recognise its importance; his mind was absorbed and distracted at the moment,—Strafford's fate hanging in the balance; and it passed almost without remark. Yet it was the hardest blow that had yet been dealt at the prerogative.

The race was maintained at the same pace till the finish. Before the political conflict closed, the King had been deprived of most of the attributes of Sovereignty—in so far as he could be deprived of them by resolutions or ordinances of a House which had ceased to be representative.

It is on Pym's pre-eminence in parliamentary tactics and counsel during the early years of the Long Parliament that his fame is mainly rested. He was no doubt animated and persuasive in debate; but can it be truly said that as a leader he played his cards with sagacity, or that as a patriot he deserves well of his country? It appears to be admitted by his warmest admirers that his intellect was not constructive, and that he had no grasp of principle. There were occasions when an able parliamentary leader might have conciliated the Church of England, united the warring sects, and possibly averted Civil War. But Pym had not the faintest apprehension of the doctrine of toleration; and any remonstrance against the fanatical intemperance of his allies was regarded by him as a high crime and misdemeanour. The Kentish petitioners received no mercy. To his treatment of their complaints the Civil War has been attributed by more than one historian. Without the Church of England, Charles would have been comparatively powerless: and it was Pym's policy that rallied the Church of England round Charles. Pym, besides, was more or less directly responsible for the unspeakable miseries of the Irish rebellion. Had he been a true statesman he would have understood that without Strafford the Irish Anarchy would revive; that if the cage were opened, and the keeper discharged, the wild beast would escape. But he had never studied the Irish problem, and he fancied that by pedantic adherence to constitutional commonplaces a mortal malady—the sore of centuries—might be healed. So he sacrificed Strafford to popular clamour and personal animosity; and within six months of Strafford's death Ireland was in convulsions.

"Oh for one hour of Dundee!" was the cry of the old Highlander who remembered the charge at Killiecrankie. Similar words must have risen to the lips of many an Irish loyalist, when he saw the smoke of burning dwellings, and heard the cries of homeless women and children, going up to Heaven. "Oh for one hour of Wentworth!" But—thanks to Pym—the strong hand and the powerful brain were no longer available.

The House of Commons was acting on the defensive. So Pym alleged. It is difficult to understand in what sense he could have used the words. Charles, when his ablest minister had been taken from him, had consented to relinquish many of the powers which had been hitherto exercised by the Sovereign. The Court of Star Chamber as well as the Court of High Commission had been abolished. So had the Council of the North. The levy of ship-money had been made illegal, and the revenue derived by the Crown from tonnage and poundage was to cease. It is hardly an exaggeration to say that in less than two years the prerogative had been stript bare. But the Commons craved for more—much more; absolute authority, both legislative and executive. They claimed to control the militia, the trained bands, the navy. The fortresses must be garrisoned by men whose fidelity to Parliament had been approved. That Grand Remonstrance, as has been said, was in substance an appeal to the people rather than an address to the Crown. It was a supplement or appendix to the "root-and-Branch" bill,—the bill by which the bishops were to be turned adrift. "We confess our intention is, and our endeavours have been, to reduce within bounds that exorbitant power which the prelates have assumed unto themselves, so contrary both to the Word of God and the laws of the land, to which end we passed the Bill for the removing them from their temporal power and employments; that so the better they might with meekness apply themselves to the discharge of their functions, which Bill themselves opposed, and were the principal instruments of crossing." But there was to be no toleration. "And we do here declare that it is far from our purpose or desire to let loose the golden reins of discipline and government in the Church, to leave private persons or particular congregations to take up what form of Divine service they please; for we hold it requisite that there should be throughout the whole realm a conformity to that order which the laws enjoin according to the Word of God. And we desire to unburden the consciences of men of needless and superstitious ceremonies, suppress innovations, and take away the monuments of idolatry. And the better to effect the intended reformation, we desire there may be a general synod of the most grave, pious, learned, and judicious divines of this island, assisted with some from foreign parts professing the same religion with us; who may consider of all things necessary for the peace and good government of the Church, and represent the results of their consultations unto the Parliament, to be there allowed and confirmed, and receive the stamp of authority, thereby to find passage and obedience throughout the kingdom."

ANNE HYDE, DUCHESS OF YORK.

From the painting by Sir Peter Lely, in the Collection of Her Majesty the Queen at Hampton Court Palace.

A Puritan Synod was to be convened, and the Episcopal Church was to taste of its tender mercies. Both in England and Ireland the Catholic religion was to be suppressed. When they would not join in demanding the control of the fortresses and the militia, the Lords were warned, "that this House being the representative body of the whole kingdom, and their Lordships being but as particular persons, and coming to Parliament in a particular capacity, that, if they should not be pleased to consent to the passing of those Acts and others necessary to the preservation and safety of the kingdom, that then this House together with such of the Lords that are more sensible of the safety of the kingdom, may join together and represent the same to His Majesty." Later on the Lords were informed that the Commons would be glad of their help and would be sorry if the story of the present Parliament should tell posterity that in so great a danger and extremity the House of Commons should be enforced to save the kingdom alone, and that the House of Peers should have no part in the honour of the preservation of it. Finally the policy of Pym was formulated in nineteen propositions which on June 3rd were sent to the King. In these the claim of Parliament to absolute sovereignty was stated with the utmost precision. The King's Council, the King's officials, the King's Guard, the judges of the Supreme Court, the officers of the militia, were to be selected by the Commons; the fortresses were to be placed in the hands of persons approved by Parliament. The laws against recusancy were to be resolutely executed. The children of Roman Catholic parents were to be educated as Protestants. The Church was to be reformed according to Puritan methods, and no new Peers were to be allowed to sit in the House of Lords without the consent of the Commons. The written remonstrance was rapidly emphasised by decisive action. Long before the Royal Standard was raised at Nottingham, a force had been despatched to Hull to overawe the loyal inhabitants, and to secure the munitions that had been collected by Charles for his Scottish expedition. Then the fleet was seized; and on the 18th of August a declaration was issued denouncing as traitors all who gave assistance to the King.

It is vain to contend that this policy, even in its earliest stage, was defensive only. It was the policy of men who had deliberately resolved to diminish the power of the Crown and to increase the power of the Commons. For the future, the King was to be "a King of Straw." That Charles's resistance was occasionally ill-advised may be frankly admitted. Though courtiers and diplomatists praised his singular self-restraint, his temper was sometimes ruffled. Soon after Strafford's execution, acting on the advice of Montrose, he went to Scotland. He was well received and hospitably entertained in the ancient capital of the Stuarts; but, from the political point of view, the visit could not be reckoned a success. Nor need it be denied that the attempt to arrest the leaders of the House (though its importance as an incident in the conflict has been unduly magnified) was a deplorable indiscretion. On the other hand Charles's fealty to the Church of England proved of infinite service to the Royal cause. "I hear," he wrote from Scotland, "it is reported that at my return I intend to alter the government of the Church of England and to bring it to the form that is here. Therefore I command you to assure all my servants that I am constant to the discipline and doctrine of the Church of England established by Queen Elizabeth and my father, and that I resolve by the grace of God to die in the maintenance of it." Once and again he had given way; but his concessions had failed to conciliate the irreconcilable Commons. "How am I to take away the bishops," he remarked to the Dutch Envoy, "having sworn at my coronation to maintain them in their privileges and pre-eminences? At the beginning I was told that all would go well if I would allow the execution of the Lord Lieutenant of Ireland; then it was if I would grant a triennial Parliament; then it was if I would allow the present Parliament to remain sitting as long as it wished; now it is if I place the ports, the Tower, and the militia in their hands; and scarcely has that request been presented when they ask me to remove the bishops. You see how far their intentions go." His constancy to the Church was duly rewarded,—as it deserved to be, for it was entirely genuine; though the conversion of the

Episcopal party into a Royalist party may have been partly due to the disfavour with which the irreverent practices of the fanatical sects began to be regarded. One half of the English people at least were still loyal to the Communion of their fathers,—were still proud of the stately and venerable Church, to which they were bound by a thousand ties. To them the "reign of the Saints" held out no prospect of peace,—it was the euphuistic equivalent for spiritual tyranny and spiritual anarchy. The Puritan divine, were he to get the upper hand, would, it was to be feared, prove no less truculent than Brownist or Familist, than Adamist or Anabaptist, than Praise-God-Bare-Bone or Prophet Hunt. The scene at Chillingworth's death-bed, at Chillingworth's grave, bore eloquent testimony to the evil fortune that was in store for England should Puritanism prevail. Chillingworth, like Falkland, had taken refuge in the King's camp; but was captured at Arundel by the Parliamentary forces. As he lay sick to death at Chichester he was visited by Francis Cheynell, one of the rigid, zealous Presbyterians "who were very unwilling that any should be suffered to go to Heaven but in the right way." This member of the Westminster Assembly gave the great latitudinarian no rest. Acting upon the words of the Apostle—"Rebuke them sharply, that they may be sound in the faith"—he plied the dying man with questions about his opinions. "I desired him," he says, "to tell me whether he conceived that a man living or dying a Turk, Papist or Socinian could be saved? All the answer I could gain from him was that he did not absolve them and would not condemn." The Westminster divine was shocked. "Sir," he said, "it is confessed that you have been very excessive in your charity. You have lavished so much charity upon Turks, Socinians, Papists, that I am afraid you have very little to spare for a truly reformed Protestant." Cheynell attended the funeral that he might throw into the open grave the great Protestant apology. "If they please" (so Cheynell proceeds) "to undertake the burial of his corpse, I shall undertake to bury his errors which are published in this so much admired yet unworthy book; and happy would it be for the Kingdom if this book and all its fellows could be so buried. Get thee gone," (he continued, throwing the volume into the open grave), "thou cursed book which has seduced so many precious souls! Get thee gone thou corrupt, rotten book! Earth to earth, and dust to dust! Get thee out into this place of rottenness, that thou mayest rot with the author, and see corruption!"

Henrietta Maria was no doubt an indiscreet adviser; she was mainly responsible for the attempt to arrest the members, as she was mainly responsible for its failure; but it is obvious that the attitude of the Long Parliament, before the outburst of the war, was offensive as well as defensive, and that it preferred claims which at whatever peril a constitutional monarch was bound to resist. On the other hand the attempt to arrest the members was the sole illegality of which Charles could be reasonably accused. He was goaded into it. What he did was done with ill-concealed reluctance. His air of sad abstraction was visible to all. He studiously avoided any show of violence. He accepted Lenthall's apology.—"May it please Your Majesty," the Speaker replied, when Charles inquired if the five members were present, "I have neither eye to see nor tongue to speak in this place but as this House is pleased to direct me,"—without a word of anger or remonstrance. "Well, well," Charles answered, "'tis no matter. I think my eyes are as good as another's." Again he looked along the benches. "Well," he said, "all the birds are flown. I do expect that you will send them to me as soon as they return hither. But I assure you on the word of a King I shall proceed against them in a fair and legal way for I never did intend any force. And now since I see I cannot do what I came for, I think this no unfit occasion to repeat what I have formerly said that whatsoever I have done for the good of my subjects I mean to maintain it."

Here again was Nemesis—the Nemesis from which the unhappy King could not escape. Lady Carlisle, shocked by Charles's betrayal of his great Minister, had gone over to the enemy. It was through her that Pym was warned in time. Before Charles had reached Westminster, the Parliamentary leaders were in the City, where among the stout apprentices of the crafts they were beyond reach of harm.

THE HOUSE OF COMMONS

From an old print, 1648.

It may be added that, before the peace was broken, no secular grievance of any consequence remained unredressed; and that the Civil War, so far as it was not a conflict between social forces—between the aristocratic Cavalier and the democratic Roundhead—must be regarded, mainly if not exclusively, as "a war of religion."

So at last in grim earnest, the War had come. There was no more room for debate. Killigrew, one of the last Royalist members who remained at Westminster, spoke out his mind quite frankly before he rode off to join the King. "If there be occasion," he said, "I will provide a good horse, and a good sword, and I make no question but I shall find a good cause."

EXECUTION OF CHARLES I.

From an old print.

## CHAPTER NINE.

### THE CIVIL WAR.

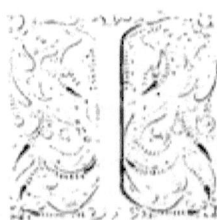

I HAVE said in a previous chapter that the crucial question when we come to weigh the relative culpability of King and Commons is,—Who was directly responsible for the outbreak of civil war? Who was truly the aggressor? I am glad to find, on turning again to Hallam, who seldom favours the King, that his view is substantially identical with that at which I had arrived. The plea that the Commons were fighting for liberty is brushed aside with scant ceremony. "How little there was of such liberty as a wise man would hold dear!" The claim of the Parliament for the control of the militia was in his judgment a claim that could not possibly be entertained by a constitutional monarch. "The notion that either, or both, Houses of Parliament, who possess no portion of executive authority, could take on themselves one of its most peculiar and important functions, was so preposterous that we can scarcely give credit to the sincerity of any reasonable person who advanced it. It is vain to deny," he continues, "that Charles had made the most valuable concessions, and such as had cost him very dear. He had succeeded, according to the judgment of many real friends of the Constitution, in putting the House of Commons in the wrong... Law, justice, moderation, once ranged against him, had gone over to his banner. His arms might reasonably be called defensive, if he had no other means of preserving himself from the condition, far worse than captivity, of a sovereign compelled to a sort of suicide upon his own honour and authority." In short Charles could not go further if he were to retain even titular authority. Hallam finds in the action of the Commons "a series of glaring violations, not only of positive and constitutional law, but of those higher principles which are paramount to all immediate policy... These great abuses of power, becoming daily more frequent as they became less excusable, would make a sober man hesitate to support them in a civil war wherein their success must not only consummate the destruction of the Crown, the Church, and the peerage, but expose all who had dissented from their proceedings, as it ultimately happened, to an oppression less severe perhaps, but far more sweeping, than that which had rendered the Star Chamber odious." And on the general charge of having caused the bloodshed of the war, upon which and not on any form of misgovernment Charles's condemnation was grounded, the historian concludes that it was as ill-established as it would have been insufficient. "Well might the Earl of Northumberland say, when the ordinance for the King's trial was before the Lords, that the greatest part of the people of England were not yet satisfied whether the King levied war first against the Houses, or the Houses against him. The fact, in my opinion, was entirely otherwise. It is quite another question

OLIVER CROMWELL.

From the painting in the Collection of the Earl of Buckinghamshire, at Hampden House

whether the Parliament were justified in their resistance to the King's legal authority. But we may contend that when Hotham by their command shut the gates of Hull against his Sovereign, when the militia was called out in different counties by an ordinance of the two Houses, both of which preceded by several weeks any levying of forces for the King, the bonds of our constitutional law were by them and their servants snapped asunder; and it would be the mere pedantry and chicane of political casuistry to enquire, even if the fact could be better ascertained, whether at Edgehill, or in the minor skirmishes that preceded, the first carbine was discharged by a Cavalier or a Roundhead. The aggressor in a war is not the first who uses force, but the first who renders force necessary."

This is as weighty an indictment as could well be penned,—especially when we consider that it was penned by an historian whose impartiality is unimpeachable. It is clear that one of the writers who up to the meeting of the Long Parliament had been well affected to the Commons, had at length found their conduct incapable of further defence. The guilt of the Civil War was theirs: they were truly responsible for the subversion of the Constitution and the prolonged anarchy that followed: the only plea that can be preferred on their behalf is that they could not trust the King. Hume in an elaborate argument has shown that the incidents on which the plea is based admit of a construction consistent with Charles's good faith; even if Hume's argument be unsound, it would not follow that the action of the Commons was justifiable, or that any grave culpability attached to the King. He had been forced sorely against his inclination into a mortal combat. It is not true that all is fair in war; but much may be forgiven to the man who is fighting for his life. We do not seriously blame the drowning sailor who clutches at any spar—however rotten.

The first Civil War began when the Standard was raised at Nottingham on August 22nd, 1642; it virtually ended at Naseby on June 14th, 1645,—though there were desultory engagements till the end of the year. We may call it therefore a three years' war. The tide of battle ebbed and flowed during these years within certain tolerably well-defined limits. Before the fighting began the Parliament men believed, or professed to believe, that one short campaign—a single battle—would convince Charles of their overwhelming superiority. Probably there were men with the King who were hardly less confident. Both were profoundly mistaken. The hostile forces, so far as we can judge, were not unequally matched. Before many weeks had passed it was found that the main strength of the Puritans lay in the Eastern and South-Eastern counties, the main strength of the King in the Northern, the South-Western and the Welsh. At one time a line drawn from Berwick-on-Tweed to the Isle of Wight would have roughly separated the districts friendly or hostile to Charles; as the Royalists waxed strong the line might have been drawn from Bridlington Bay to the Solent; as their strength waned, from Chester to Exeter along the borders of Wales. But even when the fortunes of the Puritans were at their darkest a narrow band of Parliamentary counties—Lancaster, Cheshire, Stafford, Warwick—divided the Royalist North from the Royalist South. The separation was always a grave misfortune for Charles—he was strong at York, he was strong at Oxford; but, going from one to the other, he had to pass through an enemy's country. London was the Parliamentary capital, Oxford the Royalist; but soon after the commencement of the war the great cities of Bristol, York, and Exeter declared for, or were captured by, the King; and each became a separate base of operations for the Royalists' generals. It may be said with confidence that without London the Parliament would have been powerless; and it was only on its democratic handicraftsmen and truculent apprentices that they could count with confidence. The moneyed men were mostly for the King.

Charles when he left Westminster had a scanty following. He was forced back upon the Welsh Border. But his small force was rapidly recruited and he turned upon Essex, the Parliamentary general; and the first battle of the war was fought at Edgehill on October 23rd,—an indecisive engagement owing to the impetuosity of Prince Rupert. Rupert was a younger son of the Elector Palatine, and in many ways a fit leader for the Cavaliers of England. He made a dashing captain of horse,—his cavalry charge was well nigh irresistible; but really fine military qualities were spoiled by an incurable rashness. Had he kept his men in hand, Edgehill would probably have been won, and London would have fallen at the first blow. Marston Moor was in like manner lost. So possibly was Naseby. Yet Charles could hardly have done much without Rupert to lead the way. Rupert was the inspiring spirit of the army, and in spite of his want of restraint on the battle-field he had sound sense and a keen intelligence. He was content to leave the general conduct of the campaigns to the old Scotsman, Lord Brentford, who was Charles's trusted adviser from the beginning, and whose offensive and defensive strategy had been approved by the Prince of Orange. The other great Royalist general was Hopton; and it was mainly by Hopton that the whole West of England, from the Land's End to Exeter, was recovered. Charles himself was a fairly competent soldier; and his success in the earlier campaigns was due as much to superior strategy as to the better quality of his men. It must be admitted, I think, that he bore himself well and becomingly throughout the war. He was always ready to welcome any overture for peace. He made the first advances; he would in his own words "take the honey out of the gall." Historians insist that he was unduly obstinate, and would not listen to reason. But the pretensions of the Parliament, as we have seen, were exorbitant, and it cannot be truly said that they were abated by disaster. Their claims, when battle after battle had been lost, did not differ in substance from the claims they had made before the war began. No basis for pacification could be found in such an attitude.

The propositions submitted on various occasions by the Parliament to a King, with a victorious army and a clear half of England behind him, were simply preposterous. When the tide began to turn in their favour they became more and more intolerable. Take for instance the settlement formulated in the eight propositions of November 20th, 1644. It was an ecclesiastical settlement on the basis of an intolerant Presbyterianism.

The King as well as every subject was to swear to the Covenant. It was a political settlement on the basis of a general proscription. All Papists were absolutely excluded from pardon, and fifty-seven of the noblemen and gentlemen (with the Princes Rupert and Maurice), whose loyalty had been most marked, were placed on the list of the proscribed. In short from every man who had served his King some penalty was to be exacted.

The arrogance of the Commons had no doubt its effect upon the King. "There are three things," Charles said, "I will not part with —the Church, my crown, and my friends; and you will have much ado to get them from me." And as the clouds gathered and the gloom deepened his tone and his attitude became more resolute. There is already the accent of the "martyr" in the letter I am about to quote, and in another in which he had warned his son to make no ignominious concessions even to save his father's life. "If I had any other quarrel but the defence of my religion, crown and friends, you had full reason for your advice; for I confess that speaking as a mere soldier or statesman, I must say there is no probability but of my ruin; yet, as a Christian, I must tell you that God will not suffer rebels and traitors to prosper, nor this cause to be overthrown; and whatever personal punishment it shall please Him to inflict upon me, must not make me repine, much less give over this quarrel; and there is as little question that a composition with them at this time is nothing else but a submission, which, by the grace of God, I am resolved against, whatever it cost me; for I know my obligation to be both in conscience and honour, neither to abandon God's cause, injure my successors, nor forsake my friends. Indeed I cannot flatter myself with expectation of good success more than this, to end my days with honour and a good conscience; which obliges me to continue my endeavours, as not despairing that God may yet in due time avenge His own cause; though I must aver to all my friends that he that will stay with me at this time must expect and resolve either to die for a good cause, or—which is worse—to live as miserable in maintaining it as the violence of insulting rebels can make him." At the same time there was to be no more persecution; the rights of conscience were to be respected; freedom was to be left to all persons "of what opinions soever in matters of ceremony;" and the penalties on nonconformity were to be suspended or removed.

I cannot make this a complete chronicle of the war; a bald enumeration of dates and names would be uninteresting and uninstructive: yet some of the more characteristic incidents must be briefly noted.

Mr. Gardiner has duly appreciated the superiority of the Royalist strategy in the earlier campaigns. He cannot understand indeed why it had not been attended with an even greater measure of success. "What was, in fact, really wonderful was not that Charles had accomplished so much, but that he had not accomplished more. During the three campaigns over which the war had lasted strategical superiority had been entirely on the King's side. Not only had the movements of the Royalist forces been directed in accordance with a well-conceived plan, but the plan had been varied from time to time as circumstances required. In the first short campaign, which ended at Turnham Green, the object of the person, whoever it may have been, who directed the Royal armies was to drive right at the heart of the enemy, and to deal him a mortal wound. When this proved impracticable, recourse was had in that second campaign which opened with the siege of Reading and closed with the battle of Cheriton, to a scheme in accordance with which combat was to be refused in the centre, whilst the two wings in Yorkshire and Cornwall pushed on to smother the weaker enemy between them. After this scheme, too, had been tried in vain, and when the balance of numbers had turned against Charles, the very opposite plan was tried. Abandoning the attempt to act from the circumference upon the centre, Charles resolved to act from the centre upon the circumference. Adopting the principle which was afterwards to be stamped with the mint-mark of Napoleon, he was to fling his forces first upon the Scots and their allies in Yorkshire, and then alternately upon the divided armies of the southern generals in

Oxfordshire and in Cornwall. When this was done he was to regain his position of vantage at Oxford, to wait safely there till the divisions of his adversaries gave him another opportunity."

How did it happen then that in spite of superior strategy the Royalists failed to win?

Mr. Gardiner constantly insists that Charles had no real sympathy with his people, and that to this radical defect most of the mistakes and consequently most of the disasters of his reign in peace and war were due. I am not sure that I exactly follow the argument; the evidence that there was any such gulf between the King and his subjects is certainly not convincing; in so far at least as Charles failed in the Civil War a simpler explanation will suffice.

Any comparison between the military capacity of Charles and the military capacity of Cromwell would be out of place. The materials on which to form a judgment do not perhaps exist. It would be extremely interesting to obtain the opinion of an expert like Lord Roberts or Lord Wolseley on the soldierly qualities of Oliver. Was he a great captain in the sense that Marlborough and Napoleon were great captains? Was he a master of strategy? Was he a master of tactics? Intellectual suppleness, responding readily to any emergency however unexpected, is as necessary to the leader of an army as to the leader of a senate. Was Cromwell from this point of view fitted for supreme command? These are questions which have been left unanswered. There can, I suppose, be no doubt that as a captain of cavalry he had few rivals. Rupert's headlong rush was irresistible for the moment, even more so than Cromwell's; but then Cromwell was always able to keep his men in hand. Rupert's impetuosity invited disaster, whereas Cromwell even in the thick of battle was invariably cool and wary. But if Cromwell was not a master of the art of war, if he was neither strategist nor tactician, but only an exceptionally brilliant cavalry officer, how did he win his battles?

In the first eighteen months of the war fortune inclined to the Royalists. When Arundel surrendered on December 9th, 1643, they had been winning all along the line. After that they began to decline (Marston Moor was fought on July 2nd, 1644, Naseby on June 14th, 1645). For eighteen months the superiority of the Royalists as fighting men had been maintained. Had the conditions remained unchanged to the end, Charles must have won. But their reverses had not been thrown away on the leaders of the Parliamentary forces; they wisely resolved to remodel the army. The Cavaliers, though sturdy swordsmen, were self-willed and insubordinate; and they were not happy when discipline was severe. But against the unorganised rabble of the City they were strong. Cromwell and Waller had little faith in the military prowess of idle apprentices and the waifs and strays of the streets. There must be order and there must be godliness. A regiment of disciplined enthusiasts would be of more service than a battalion of disorganised and dissolute mercenaries. There was abundance of spiritual fervour and visionary exaltation in the South-Eastern counties, which a drill sergeant who understood his business might mould into an "army of the Lord." A secular war must be turned into a Crusade; and the Crusaders must be men who not only feared God, but kept their powder dry.

It is easy to understand how irresistible an argument on a battle-field such a force must have proved. It was hard as granite, keen as steel. Into the gallant but disorderly ranks of the Cavaliers a solid wedge was driven. The zealot who is fighting his way to Heaven has nothing to fear. If he kills his man, as poor young Walton said, when he was dying on Marston Moor, he is "the executioner of God upon his enemies" (to such bitterness between brothers life in a model Puritan household had grown); if he is killed "the brief minute's fierce annoy" cannot compare with "God's eternity of Joy." With such a weapon in his hand, even had his enemy been a trained and experienced veteran—a Tilly or Spinola—Cromwell could hardly have failed to win. But he fought against simple rustics led by country gentlemen to whom the art of war was a mystery. Since Cromwell's time we have had constant wars in Asia and Africa; and everywhere handfuls of highly disciplined British soldiers have held their own against hosts of savage foes. Mighty waves have broken upon it; but the British square has stood firm. The fact that Cromwell was on the winning side at Marston Moor and Naseby and Worcester and Drogheda cannot therefore be held to prove that he was a great general. The marvel indeed would have been had he failed to win. I confess that to my ear more than one of the despatches which after victory he wrote from the battle-field, and which by Mr. Carlyle's magic have been translated into martial melodies, do not ring true. "This is the Lord's doing; it is marvellous in our eyes!" *That* is the refrain; but the writer is careful to show that no one except the Lord—no meaner ally—had any share in the victory of the Ironsides. Douce David Lesley and his canny Scots, after their hard fight on the Moor at Marston, are studiously slighted. "Truly England and the Church of God have had a great favour from the Lord in this great victory given unto us, such as the like never was since this war began. It had all the evidences of an absolute victory obtained by the Lord's blessing upon the godly party principally. We never charged but we routed the enemy. The left wing which I commanded, being our own horse, *saving a few Scots in our rear,* beat all the Prince's horse. God made them as stubble to our swords. We charged their regiments of foot with our horse, and routed all we charged." Again it is difficult to listen with patience to his language after Naseby. "I can say this of Naseby that when I saw the enemy draw up and march in gallant order towards us, and we a company of poor ignorant men, to seek how to order our battle, the general having commanded me to order all the horse, I could not—riding alone about my business—but smile out to God in praises in assurance of victory, because God would *by things that are not bring to nought things that are* of which I had great assurance—and God did it." Mr. Gardiner has made a careful calculation of the numbers on either side, from which it appears that Fairfax had 14,000 men on the field as against Rupert's 7,500; and he adds: "After all, a victory in which 14,000 men defeated 7,500, and that too not without difficulty, cannot be reckoned amongst the great examples of military efficiency." In these circumstances, however, it had been made clear to Cromwell that God would by things that are not (Fairfax's 14,000) bring to nought things that are (Rupert's 7,500). If this is not cant, what is it? No one now denies that Carlyle sometimes mistook a sham heroism, a sham godliness, for the genuine article.

Cromwell was undoubtedly a highly efficient drill sergeant as well as a competent cavalry officer,—though it has been asserted that to Waller the credit of re-organising the parliamentary army was really due, and that Rupert was the author of the system of cavalry tactics which has been commonly associated with Cromwell's name. It was from Waller no doubt that the first suggestion of the New Model came; and, if Waller's description of the army which he had been leading is not extravagantly overcharged, it was certainly time that a change were made. "Such men," he concludes emphatically, "are only fit for a gallows here, and a hell hereafter." But Cromwell probably had spoken quite as plainly to Hampden. "*Your* troops are most of them old decayed serving-men and tapsters and such kind of fellows, and *their* troops are gentlemen's sons and persons of quality. Do you think that the spirits of such base and mean fellows will ever be able to encounter gentlemen that have honour, and courage, and resolution in them?" By whomsoever brought about, however, the transformation was notable. The "Ironsides" were a peculiar people. Rupert with his touch of genius invented the name,—after his defeat at Marston Moor he applied it to Cromwell. But it came to mean much more than it meant to Rupert. It meant a political as well as a military force,—a vast social confederacy where martial law was severely enforced; a noisy debating club where any infraction of military discipline was instantly punished. Nothing exactly like it had been known before. The presbyterian Richard Baxter, who was an army chaplain, has left a vivid record of his experiences. These illiterate mechanics were framing for themselves a new heaven and a new earth. The wildest political speculations were freely ventilated. The grossest religious delusions were frankly tolerated, if not openly encouraged. Military saints who had "seen visions and revelations" mounted the pulpits, and "godly precious men, who had filled dung carts before they were captains," expounded the Word. In the eyes of these men no sacredness attached to the person of King or Priest. "I perceived," says Baxter, "they took the King for a tyrant and an enemy, and really intended to master him or to ruin him, and they thought if they might fight against him they might kill or conquer him. They plainly showed me," he continues, "that they thought God's providence would cast the trust of religion and the kingdom upon them as conquerors; they made nothing of all the most wise and godly in the armies and garrisons that were not of their way." A thoroughly disciplined army with a distinct sectarian impress could not but prove dangerous to the independence of laymen; and Cromwell had never disguised that he was forging an instrument which he meant to use for political ends. "I will not deny," he said to Manchester, "but that I desire to have none in my army but such as are of the Independent judgment." Manchester asked his reason for so unusual a resolution. "That in case," replied Cromwell, "there should be propositions for peace, or any other conclusion of a peace, such as might not stand with the ends that honest men should aim at, *this army might prevent such a mischief*." He was trying a dangerous experiment. It has been truly said that no solid political edifice can be raised upon a merely military foundation; and in this case the military foundation was composed of bigoted zealots who were ignorant of the first principles of government. What kind of *Civitas Dei* were such men competent to rear? Cromwell might call himself their master; but he would be at their mercy. He could not help himself; their policy must be his. And a policy that would last could not be moulded by illiterate craftsmen. It was a grave disaster that the attempt should have been made; for it had all to be undone—all at least that was not on the sure lines of constitutional development. The "transcendent, extraordinary, miraculous light" to which they trusted was a Will-o'-the-wisp.

"This brave army is our violets and primroses, the first fruits of the spring, which the Parliament sends forth this year for the growth of our religion, and the re-implanting of this kingdom in the garden of peace and truth." So a Puritan writes; and the Puritans were justly proud of their New Model--the army which Cromwell and Waller had reorganised, and by which the local militia and trained bands had been replaced. But it may fairly be doubted whether, even when purged of its baser elements, the Parliamentary army by itself could have effectually arrested the Royalist advance. *Without the co-operation of the Scots they could hardly have won.* Before the Scots were called in, even the capital was in revolt. More than once the cry for peace could not be silenced. "Peace and truth!" called out some one who took the unpopular side, at a tumult in the market-place. "Hang truth! let us have peace at any price!" was the reply. There had always been a large Royalist minority among the substantial citizens; and even the enforced subscription of the Covenant had only secured outward conformity. "Scarce one man in a hundred," a shrewd observer wrote, "throughout all London but hath subscribed to it. I find notwithstanding by discourse that the greatest part of the people are little weaned from the present Service-Book, and wish better to Episcopacy a little reformed rather than Presbyterial or any other Church government whatsoever." The moderate Puritans were very averse to appeal for aid to the Scots (and their disinclination was shared, then and later, by Cromwell); but, the absolute necessity for Scottish succour becoming apparent, scruples were discarded, and the Scots army which crossed the Tweed on January 19th, 1644, became an important factor in the subsequent conflict.

It cannot be said that any of the battles of the campaign are particularly interesting. No fight stands out from the rest with special distinctness or distinction. There is a good deal of luck, good or bad as the case may be, on either side: one half of a battle is won, one half is lost, and the combatants are as they were. Several conflicts are memorable mainly for the men who fell at them—Hampden at Chalgrove, Falkland at Newbury, Sir Bevil Grenvile at Lansdowne. Hampden riding away, bowed over his saddle in mortal agony, from the fatal field; Falkland spurring his horse through the murderous gap in the hedge to meet the rain of bullets and the death he coveted; Sir Bevil struck down in the moment of victory with his hardy Cornishmen round him on the slippery ledge they had won; are striking figures. These were the men who on either side gave a distinction to this miserable contest. It was because men like Sir Bevil were true to the King that the Royalist cause prospered as it did. The Roundheads when they counted on an easy victory had failed to reckon with these country gentlemen. No discouragement could shake a loyalty which was bred in the bone. "I cannot contain myself within doors," the famous Cornishman wrote, "when the King of England's standard waves in the field upon so just an occasion; the cause being such as must make all those that die in it little inferior to martyrs. I am not without consideration, as you lovingly advise, of my wife and family; and as for her, must acknowledge that she hath ever drawn so evenly in the yoke with me as she hath never pressed before, nor hung behind me, nor ever opposed nor resisted my will: and yet truly I have not in this or anything else endeavoured to walk in any way of power with her but of reason; and though her love will submit to either, yet truly my respect will not suffer me to urge my power unless I can convince by reason." Sir Bevil is one of the few historical figures which still evoke a passionate local regard,—a regard which has found fit expression in the Vicar of Morwenstow's stirring lines:—

"Ride! Ride! with red spur, there is death in delay,
'Tis a race for dear life with the devil;
If dark Cromwell prevail and the King must give way
This earth is no place for Sir Beville.

"So at Stamford he fought, and at Lansdowne he fell,
But vain were the visions he cherished:
For the great Cornish heart, that the King loved so well,
In the grave of the Granville it perished."

Saving Cromwell and Waller in the Parliamentary camp, Rupert and Hopton in the Royalist, few of the leaders were men of mark. Essex

DEATH WARRANT OF CHARLES I

From the original document, in the Library of the House of Lords

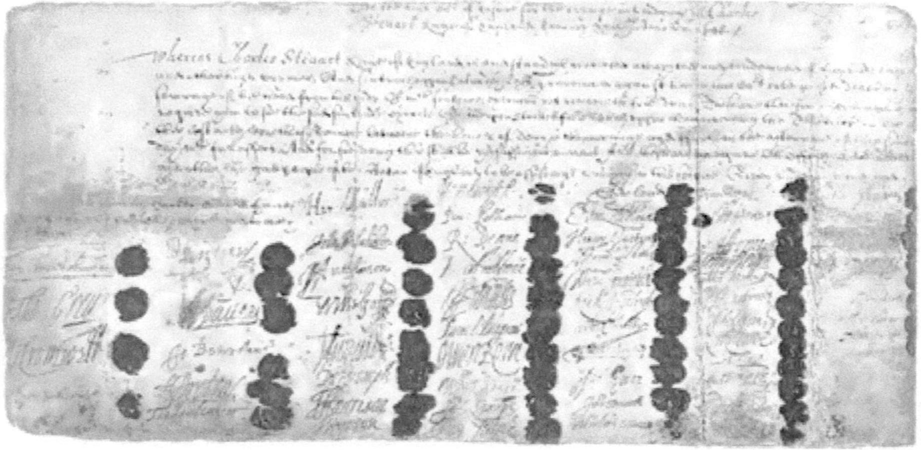

Whereas Charles Steuart

and Manchester and Newcastle are singularly colourless lay figures, entirely out of place in such a desperate struggle. Hopton, so far as I can judge, was the strongest of all the Royalist captains,—a man of military genius and powerful character. On the other side, Sir William Waller was the ablest strategist. Waller attracts as Falkland attracts. Though a consummate soldier he was urgent for peace; "I am so heartily weary of this war," he wrote, "that I shall submit to anything that may conduce to the despatch of it;" and his letters are those of a high-minded and scrupulous gentleman. Here is the one in which he declines Hopton's proposal for a private interview. "Certainly my affections to you are so unchangeable that hostility itself cannot violate my friendship to your person. But I must be true to the cause wherein I serve. The old limitation, *usque ad aras*, holds still, and where my conscience is interested all other obligations are swallowed up. I should most gladly wait upon you, according to your desire, but I look upon you as engaged in that party beyond the possibility of a retreat, and consequently incapable of being wrought upon by any persuasions. And I know the conference could never be so close between us but that it would take wind, and receive a construction to my dishonour. That great God who is the searcher of my heart knows with what a sad sense I go on upon this service, and with what a perfect hatred I detest this war without an enemy; but I look upon it as sent from God, and that is enough to silence all passion in me. The God of Heaven in His good time send us the blessing of peace, and in the meantime assist us to receive it! We are both upon the stage, and must act such parts as are assigned us in this tragedy. Let us do it in a way of honour and without personal animosities." How fine this is! hardly to be surpassed by any letter in the language—the modest expression of the humane and cultivated intelligence—Puritan it may be, but with no twang of the conventicle!

In these earlier battles Cromwell took little part. Complaint was made of his inaction at the second battle of Newbury; but at Marston Moor and

Naseby he was in the thick of the fight. What we see and hear of him otherwise is not uncharacteristic. It must be said for Cromwell that he had no pedantic regard for consistency. To maintain a reputation for consistency, for instance, at the cost of a capable recruit, was not to be thought of! A military dictator is in one sense the most absolute of rulers; but he has to study and reflect the moods of the men who have raised him to power. Oliver was the spokesman of the army to England and to Europe; and, though the convictions of the Ironsides were tolerably steady, great masses of men are apt to be moved, as the sea is moved, by any breath of wind. In Oliver we find the same curious union of speculative tolerance and practical intolerance which we find in the army which he formed. On March 10th, 1645, he wrote to Major-General Crawford, in the language of a statesman: "Surely you are not well advised thus to turn off one so faithful to the cause and so able to serve you as this man is. Sir, the State in choosing men to serve it, takes no notice of their opinions: if they be willing faithfully to serve it—that satisfies. I advised you formerly to bear with men of different minds from yourself. If you had done it when I advised you to it, you would not have had so many stumbling blocks in your way. Take heed of being sharp, or too easily sharpened by others, against whom you can object little, but that they square not with you in every matter concerning matters of religion." On January 10th of the same year he had given passionate expression, on the other hand, to his own private repugnances. Entering Ely Cathedral he ordered a clergyman who persisted in using the "choir service" to desist from so "unedifying and offensive" a practice. The clergyman refused; and Cromwell, who was governor of the Isle of Ely, went out and returned presently with a guard of soldiers. "Leave off your fooling and come down," was the peremptory order, and the service was thereupon brought to an end.

More than one of the Royalist ladies are still visible to us through the smoke of battle and oblivion;—stout, and spirited, and worthy of the absent lords who have left the great houses in their keeping—Charlotte de la Trémouille, Countess of Derby, who held Latham for three months (till relieved by Rupert) against an overwhelming force of Roundheads; Lady Sophia Murray, who when brought up for examination before the Committee of Safety, told them flatly: "I do not mean to give any account to such fellows as you are." But the Queen herself took the foremost place in every service of peril. A woman of supreme energy, she was never idle. On land or on water, she was equally in her element. Under the hottest fire of the enemy, or in the wildest winter weather, she proved herself the daughter of Henry of Navarre. On one occasion, we are told, she lay tossing for nine days on the boisterous North Sea. Never losing the high spirits which accompanied her in every position in which she was placed, she laughed heartily at the fears of her attendant ladies. "Comfort yourselves, my dears," she said, "Queens of England are never drowned." The Commons were furious; they framed a Bill of Attainder; had they caught her, she would have gone the way that Strafford and Laud had gone. He must be a churl, indeed, who refuses to recognise the heroic and untiring energy of Henrietta.

In this first Civil War there is indeed one brilliant soldier who never fails to acquit himself with distinction. Montrose was the Scottish Falkland. When he entered public life he felt that the popular liberties were in peril; and like Falkland and Strafford he took the popular side. But as soon as the suspicion crossed his mind that Argyle and the confederates were playing the King false, that they were aiming at political change rather than religious liberty, he quitted them at once and finally.

The Scottish campaign of 1644-1645 is an episode complete in itself; and may easily be detached from the rest of this rather sombre epic. It throws a sunset radiance over Charles's sinking fortunes; it is the sole gleam of light in what is thereafter one of those "sad stories of the death of Kings," which are monotonously tragic, and on which the historian is loath to linger. Though it came too late sensibly to affect the issue of the war, it was the Loyalist's most romantic and picturesque adventure, and it was conducted by one in whose career Drummond of Hawthornden welcomed "the return of the Golden Age," and of whom it was said by De Retz that he was the only man "who has ever realized to me the idea of certain ancient heroes."

It is difficult to keep pace with Montrose through that brief and brilliant campaign,—his marches are so swift and silent, his victories so rapid and dazzling. He has vowed to bring Scotland back to the King, and he begins the enterprise with a single follower. Beset on every side, he turns, and doubles, and beats back; and then, when least looked for, falls on his prey with a hawk-like swoop. He routs the solid burghers of Perth at Tippermuir; a day or two thereafter he enters the good town of Aberdeen; then, having enticed Argyle to the Spey, he plunges amid the wilds of Badenoch into outer darkness, as Mr. Carlyle would say. He is gaining time,—time to marshal the forces of the Royalists who are everywhere scattered and disheartened, and to make victory, though marvellous, not a miracle. So he reappears in Athol; reappears in Aberdeen; seats himself with consummate skill and coolness among the woods of Fyvie, where the Covenanting armies surge against him in vain. But the Gordons are sulky and will not rise; it is hopeless to wait longer in Buchan; so shaking his unwieldy enemy easily off, he once more, in the dead of winter, startles with the tread of armed men the eyries of Badenoch, and the stony watershed of the Spey.

That autumn and winter were certainly not propitious to the Puritans. At no time was there greater need for the prayer which Principal Baillie put up, that "the Almighty might be pleased to *blink* in mercy upon Scotland." What between the Papistical Highlanders of "James Graeme, sometime Marquis of Montrose," and the great storm of snow which then covered the country, the members of the Northern Presbyteries are sorely beset. But worse fortune is in store for their leaders. Argyle, much perplexed in mind by the unaccountable eccentricities of this Will-o'-the-wisp enemy, is on his way to Perth, when he learns that his rival is at his back. Seized with sudden panic, he disbands his army, and makes for the metropolis. Even there he does not feel that he is safe; so he renders up his commission to the rebel government, and flies to his inaccessible stronghold on Loch Fyne. "It's a far cry to Lochow;" and Gillespie Grumach may at length breathe freely; for his antagonist, wiry and virulent though he be, cannot follow him here. But he does not know his man. Montrose is inexorable; through the wildest passes in the bleak December storms—and it is a bitter winter—he forces his way; and on the hill-sides above his own castle Argyle again beholds the watch-fires of his foe. Craven always, and now utterly unnerved, he flies shamefully, and leaves the ruthless hunter to harry his lair.

Having sacked the country of the Campbells, Montrose plunges into Lochaber, and prepares to winter upon the desolate shores of Loch Ness. This is the critical moment, the turning-point in the campaign. He is deserted by a large proportion of his men, and on all sides surrounded by the enemy. Seaforth is in the north at Inverness; Baillie at Perth; Argyle, recovering from his panic, raises his clan, and writes to his friends in Edinburgh that he has "overtook the rogues at Lochaber." A daring blow is required. Montrose doubles back: leads his men right across the precipitous spurs of Ben Nevis; and, with startling suddenness, closes in on Macallum More and his men, who are camped round their castle of Inverlochy on the shore of Loch Eil. Argyle again, like a hunted stag, takes to the water, but he cannot take his army with him; and Auchinleck, "a stout soldier, but a very vicious man," as his Covenanting allies describe him, is left in command. The winter morning dawns, still, clear, and frosty; the Campbells can hear distinctly the flourish of trumpets that salutes the Royal standard on the mountain, and the wild war-tune of the Camerons as they quit their cover: "Come to me and I will give you flesh:" a promise that day duly kept. It was a splendid charge—a handful upon a host; it must have come back, one may guess, on Charles Napier's memory, the morning of Meeanee.

Inverlochy was the most terribly complete of Montrose's victories,—the Campbells being literally driven into the sea,—and its effect was instantaneous. The prestige of Argyle is destroyed. The Gordon cavalry, headed by the noblest gentleman of their race, join the Royal standard. The army of the Northern rebels melts away in a night. Montrose marches through Aberdeenshire and Moray into the Mearns without seeing a foe. Neither Baillie nor Hurry will fight, and "the Graeme" with masterly rapidity pushes past them to sack Dundee, from which town he effects a still more rapid and masterly retreat upon Glen Esk. The hills form a citadel where he knows that he is safe. These sterile regions are his arsenals. The Lowland cavalry dare not follow him through the passes. Thenceforth for weeks and months he becomes obscure, impalpable, veiled in darkness, a sort of terrible myth. Rumours may reach the Covenanting generals from Athol, from Loch Katrine, from Ben Lomond; not to be relied on, however, for the Puritan spies are baffled and at fault. So Hurry marches towards Inverness to join the Northmen, who are again in the field; but Montrose is forthwith upon his trail, and at Alderne, in a stiff and well-contested fight, the veteran army perishes. Baillie, advancing cautiously along the southern bank of the Spey, keeps the Royal force in sight for several days, till the Marquis again eludes him, and the scent is lost amid the woods of Abernethy. At length at Alford, in Strathdon, the two generals finally encounter; and although young Lord Gordon is slain, —a heavy and distressful blow,—Baillie is utterly routed. Of all the Covenanting armies only one now remains to be dealt with; and among the thickets of Kilsyth, Montrose wins his last, perhaps his most memorable victory. He has fulfilled his promise. From Inverness to the Border the Royal authority is re-established,—he has brought Scotland back to the King.

To do what Montrose did, to win successive victories over seven or eight trained armies, each of them superior in numbers, discipline, and organisation to that which he led, must be counted no small achievement; but the peculiar difficulty which he had to meet, and which none but a really great man could have met with success, resulted from the peculiar constitution of his own army. The Highlander was brave, and he liked fighting. But he liked plunder better, and he liked to secure his plunder.

So that the general was placed in a singular dilemma. Whenever he gained a battle, he lost his army. The victor, in the hour of victory, was left at the mercy of the vanquished. It is assuredly not the least remarkable fact in Montrose's career, that he contrived to secure permanent and enduring results, in effect, to subdue and reclaim the whole of Scotland, with an army that continually melted away, and to which victory for the day was, in truth, more destructive than defeat. Any energetic Celtic robber could issue from the passes, harry the plain, reive the black cattle of his Lowland neighbours, and then retire swiftly with the spoil into his mountain lair. He could do this; it was all that he could do. Montrose, through the felicity and daring of his genius, contrived to make these fickle and inconstant instruments work out a great scheme of national liberation. For though the body dissolved like the snow, the spirit, the *man*, remained,—a man who acted as a magnet, who drew soldiers out of every valley through which he passed, at whose war-cry the red-shanks gathered together from their remotest hills. Such a man was a nucleus, a centre, a rallying-point; and so long as their dreaded enemy lived, the rebel government felt that its supremacy in Scotland was not secure.

When, on his way to England, he is at last worsted, forced to quit his own country, and take refuge at a foreign Court, he is not cast down nor depressed. He is still fertile in expedients; still prompt, resolute and hopeful; still gentle, true, and of a good conscience. The elastic vigour of his mind is as noticeable in adversity as in victory. Charles's death indeed stung him very sorely; he felt it keenly; perhaps he was never quite the old man after it; probably it prompted that wild descent from the Orkneys, when he came back with the King's standard in black, and *nil medium* upon his own.

During the war the Parliament continued to sit; but its authority was on the wane. Even before the close of the first Civil War, the "Rump," in the opinion of the army, was beginning to lag, to wax faint, to weary in well doing. The members still occupied themselves with the suppression of "erroneous opinions, ruinating schism, and damnable heresies;"

but the sword of the Lord and of Gideon was no longer wielded with the same vigour and relish. They might issue orders for the destruction of the marvels of medieval art; and the pictures of great masters might be torn from their frames, and cast into the river; but the salt had lost its savour. Even the execution of the aged Archbishop was not a marked success. Why after keeping him secluded in the Tower for so many months, where he did and could do no harm, they should have thought it necessary to cut off the old man's head, does not clearly appear. It looks to us now like the merest wantonness,—a Puck-like vindictiveness. There were sternly logical sectaries indeed who argued that Heaven had been defrauded when Laud's life was spared and Strafford's taken. "Certainly the sparing of him hath been a great provocation to Heaven, for it is a sign that we have not been so careful to give the Church a sacrifice as the State. We could soon avenge our own injuries upon Strafford, but we have been slow and behind in revenging the cause of God upon Canterbury." Charles, for his part, trusted that his share in the shedding of innocent blood would now be forgiven. "Nothing," he wrote to Henrietta, "can be more evident than that Strafford's innocent blood hath been one of the great causes of God's just judgment upon this nation by a furious civil war, both sides hitherto being almost equally guilty; but now this last crying blood being totally theirs, I believe it is no presumption hereafter to hope that the hand of justice must be heavier upon them and lighter upon us."

But it was not to be. The hope was futile. When Charles, on the night of April 27th, 1646, stole away from Oxford, the game had been played out. More than one bloody battle indeed in yet another ill-omened campaign was to be fought; but the Civil War had virtually closed. The King had lost. Yet though the King had lost, the Commons had failed to win. They were responsible for the wreck of the Constitution; but the fruits of victory were to be reaped by others. The "godly party," with Oliver at its head, had come between them and the prize.

The rest of the story need not detain us for any time. Abortive intrigues and futile diplomacies have ceased to interest the modern reader. I need only indicate the general lines on which they proceeded. When he rode away from Oxford, Charles might have tried to leave the country. He might possibly have got across the Channel. There would have been imminent risk of capture; but he had numerous friends on the coast, and there were those among his opponents who for various reasons would have been well pleased to facilitate his escape. If he elected to remain, he might approach the Parliament, the Army, or the Scots. There was a general sense of puzzle and bewilderment; men did not know what to make of the new order of things; as representing the ancient monarchy Charles was still a power in the State. His alliance was, or might be, valuable. The Army had become, or was becoming, the controlling authority; but the Parliament was not altogether powerless as yet; and the Scots had views of their own which they were indisposed to surrender. It would have been the business of an energetic diplomatic agent to have taken advantage of the political discord to promote the progress of the party for which he acted, to play the Independent against the Presbyterian, and the Scot against one or other, or both. The charge against Charles is, I presume, that being the national Sovereign he had no right to play the part of the partisan diplomatist. The purist is probably in the right. It would have been far better had the King acted openly throughout the negotiations. Had he said frankly that whatever he did must be approved by the nation, and not by a faction only, he might have made the best terms, the best bargain, for the Crown within his power.

Charles elected to go to the Scots camp which was then before Newark. The Scots had informally intimated their desire to come to terms with him; but he might have known that the question of religion would present an insuperable barrier. They were fanatical Presbyterians far more fanatical than the English; and Charles's obstinate loyalty to the Anglican Church never wavered. Even as a fugitive he would consent to no compromise that would permanently disable her. "How can I keep my innocency which you, with so much reason oft and earnestly persuade me to preserve, if I should abandon the Church? Believe it, religion is the only firm foundation of all power; that cast loose or depraved, no government can be stable; for when was there ever obedience where religion did not teach it? But, which is most of all, how can we expect God's blessing if we relinquish His Church? And I am most confident that religion will much sooner regain the militia than the militia will religion." He would probably have fared better had he trusted himself to one or other of the English parties. The continued presence of a Scots Army in England (when the war had ceased) was on all hands viewed with disfavour; and when it was found that the King was in their camp the desire to be rid of this flock of locusts naturally grew. Nor were the Scots unwilling to go. They had eaten up the Northern counties. If they could get their bill settled, there was no reason why they should remain. But what was to be done with Charles? Mr. Gardiner argues that it cannot be justly charged against the Scots that they sold their King for £400,000. It is certainly not correct to say that the Scots sold Charles as Judas sold Jesus; it would be nearer the mark to say that they held him as a "material guarantee" for payment of the debt due to them by the English Parliament. It does not admit of doubt that the possession of Charles's person tended, to say the least, to a prompt settlement of accounts. Unless they had got paid the Scots would not have retired; unless they had got Charles the English would not have paid, at least till later.

On the retirement of the Scots Charles was sent by the Parliament to Holmby House, in Northamptonshire. But the controversy between Parliament and Army becoming acute, the Independent leaders deemed it wiser that Charles should be in their own hands, and Lieutenant Joyce with a troop of Ironsides authorized by Cromwell, carried him off to Newmarket. Thereafter, while the differences became more and more accentuated, he was mainly in the custody of the Independents.

What was to come of it all? In whom, now that the Constitution had been wrecked, was authority to be vested anew? No basis of intellectual compromise had as yet been found,—no basis of intellectual compromise, nor indeed of simplest *modus vivendi!* There was no possible makeshift—the ruts were too deep. The anarchy had come, which only the strong hand of a military dictator could compose. When the strong hand was removed, it was to be hoped that the nation would drift back into the old paths realizing at the same time that the old paths required periodical renewal and repair.

In the meantime the virtue mainly required from Royalists, and from others than Royalists, was *patience*. Premature action would be pernicious. Hence it was an enormous mistake when the civil conflict was renewed by the Scots. Charles and his allies should have learned to wait. Time was on their side. It would have been seen more and more clearly when the heated brains began to cool that any real progress towards a permanent settlement must be on monarchical lines. The second Civil War, imprudently and impatiently entered upon, was thus a fiasco. The Scots at Preston were as sheep in the hands of the butcher. Moreover it gave the "godly party" in the Army the pretext that it desired. What was the good of negotiating with a faithless King? Better be done, once and for all, with sham conventions. While the war infuriated the Puritan army, it estranged their leader, who could lose his temper on provocation, or without provocation when it appeared desirable. That "man of blood Charles Stuart" must go *ad patres*. So before the close of January, 1648/1649, a warrant in these terms, signed by Cromwell and others was issued.

"TO COLONEL FRANCIS HACKER, COLONEL HUNCKS, AND LIEUTENANT-COLONEL PHAYR, AND TO EVERY OF THEM.

"At the High Court of Justice for the Trying and Judging of Charles Stuart, King of England, 29th January, 1648.

"WHEREAS Charles Stuart, King of England, is and standeth convicted, attainted and condemned of High Treason and other high Crimes; and Sentence upon Saturday last was pronounced against him by this Court, To be put to death by the severing of his head from his body: of which Sentence execution yet remaineth to be done:

"These are therefore to will and require you to see the said Sentence executed, in the open Street before Whitehall, upon the morrow, being the Thirtieth day of this instant month of January, between the hours of Ten in the morning and Five in the afternoon, with full effect. And for so doing, this shall be your warrant.

"And these are to require all Officers and Soldiers, and others the good People of this Nation of England, to be assisting unto you in this service.

"Given under our hands and seals.

"John Bradshaw,
"Thomas Grey (Lord Groby),
"Oliver Cromwell."
(and Fifty-six others.)

All the incidents of the scene at Whitehall have been scanned with untiring industry. Even within our own time, we have made closer acquaintance with some not unimportant details; but to repeat for the hundredth time the story of an outrage which shocked the world, and for which no apology can be offered, would be unprofitable. Charles died as the Stuarts died,—as gentle and simple had learned to die in those days of block and scaffold.

"He nothing common did or mean
Upon that memorable scene,
But with his keener eye
The axe's edge did try;
Nor called the gods with vulgar spite
To vindicate his helpless right,
But bowed his comely head
Down, as upon a bed."

A bird's-eye view is often convenient and I venture to recapitulate with extreme brevity the argument for the English Kings of the Royal House of Stuart which in this volume, and in earlier volumes, I have ventured to submit for consideration. Any argument that does not affirm the divine right of the democracy to govern is now derided; yet as Mr. Traill says "the time that has passed since the revolution

EXECUTION OF CHARLES I

From the painting by Weesop, in the Collection of the Earl of Rosebery at Dalmeny

of 1688 is short indeed in comparison with the antecedent period during which our own and other European nations had been growing steadily in strength and cohesion under systems which, with whatever admixture of the popular element, were in the main systems of personal rule."

When a Scottish prince ascended the English throne, Scotland was jubilant. The stubborn determination to remain free had never been overcome, and had now won its reward. The ancient prophecies had come true. The War of Independence had not been fought in vain. Under no other conditions, indeed, so far as one can judge, could Union have been peacefully brought about. The jealous susceptibilities of the weaker people were allayed. A Stuart King took the place of Tudor and Plantagenet: and through good and evil fortune Scotland as a whole had been true to the Stuarts. A resolute and disciplined minority, indeed, had driven Mary into exile; but, even in her lowest estate, she had failed to alienate the affectionate fidelity of two-thirds of her people. The nation at large, it is now generally admitted, was at no time hostile to her. As it was a small band of Independents with Cromwell at their head who put Charles I. to death, so it was a small band of Calvinists with Knox at their head who banished Mary. And even when Mary was banished, the rights of her infant son had been scrupulously protected. It seemed a wonderful stroke of luck that made the ruler of a petty province and an impoverished people the sovereign of a rich and prosperous empire: but the seeming gain was possibly a real loss. In spite of his personal eccentricities, James VI. had been fairly popular with the Scots: but when he crossed the Border, the frivolous pedantry and clownish gait of the wisest fool in Christendom could not fail to excite the ridicule of a polished society. Under the fierce light that beat about the English throne the womanish weaknesses of the modern Solomon—"Solomon the Son of David"—were sharply and grotesquely accentuated. The initial misunderstanding was never entirely healed. It is possible that the English people did not understand the Stuarts; it is certain that the Stuarts did not understand the English people. In Scotland no steady popular pressure had been brought to bear upon the sovereign. He enjoyed, as a rule, complete freedom of action,—doing what was right in his own eyes, until the nobles were gravely displeased, when they rose in arms and put him to death. Parliamentary opposition was practically unknown,—what resistance there was, though violent, being intermittent and spasmodic. But in England, from an almost unknown antiquity and by an almost unbroken tradition, the people had been taught to shelter their political liberties and their civic privileges behind the forms of the Constitution. No tax could be levied except with the consent of the Commons; no citizen could be punished except by legal process. The most imperious of the Tudors did not venture to cross the line that inveterate and immemorial usage had drawn; and he knew by an inherited instinct how far he could safely go. On the other hand, the whole domain of English constitutional law was a *terra incognita* to James and to his son. It might be said for them (were it any excuse) that they knew not what they did. The principles which were most deeply rooted in the convictions of Englishmen were unintelligible to rulers who had been educated abroad. So Charles entered upon a hopeless contest with a light heart. It is possible that the wisest ruler could not ultimately have averted the conflict. There were theories in the air which made all government impossible. Religion had reacted upon politics; and the Puritan had become the Republican. The sharp antagonism between the men who declared that they would live as their fathers had lived, would believe as their fathers had believed, would worship as their fathers had worshipped, and the men who hated the Church and detested the Monarchy, was certain sooner or later to bring Cavalier and Roundhead into deadly conflict. But although sooner or later an appeal to arms might have been inevitable, it was the character of the King that precipitated the crisis. In so far as he did not himself lead, he was led by Laud and Strafford. Laud appears to have been insensate and mole-like; but Wentworth was a man of quick intelligence and profound policy. It is foolish to condemn such a man without a hearing—as most historians have been inclined to do. We may be tolerably sure that he saw more than we are able to see now. He may have felt, and felt truly, that the revolution in men's minds which had taken place, which was taking place, must lead to anarchy. He may have felt, and felt truly, that the revolutionary forces could only be kept in check by rapid and decisive action, and that procrastination would be fatal to the monarchy. Had he succeeded in crushing the Revolution he might possibly have been reckoned a far-seeing English statesman; but he failed, and in such circumstances failure cannot be condoned.

To attribute the failure of the Royalists, however, to the bad faith of the King is to confound cause and effect. Charles was placed in a position in which, try as he might, he could not be consistent. He was in the centre of irresistible forces. We do not blame the cork which is tossed to and fro in the whirlpool for inconsistency; and Charles was virtually as little of a free agent. He was fighting with both hands for dear life; and if he made concessions the one day, and retracted them the next, he possibly could not help himself. So far as we can judge now, the most perfect candour, the most scrupulous rectitude, would have led to the same conclusion. The stars in their courses were fighting against the King; and neither courage nor virtue could have effectively resisted the military genius of Cromwell.

In patient courage, indeed, Charles was not deficient; and his kingly bearing upon the scaffold at Whitehall may possibly have saved the monarchy. The Stuarts at least could die well. They might be as weak and vicious in their lives as their enemies held them to be; but when they came to the end the strain of nobleness in their blood asserted itself nobly. It may be true that the execution of Charles was regretted by Cromwell; the deed which struck Europe dumb may have been forced upon him by the austere zealots whom he led; but in any view, it was a grievous blunder an immense mistake. The impression it made was indelible. The Usurper was a wise and just and vigorous ruler; but he was forced, willingly or unwillingly, to rule by the sword. The bloody stain on his escutcheon could not be wiped out. It isolated him; it alienated the moderate men in either camp; the great mass of his countrymen were scandalised by this unprecedented, this tremendous departure from constitutional methods; and, except for the army, he stood alone. Had the "Royal martyr" been permitted to die in his bed, Cromwell might have been the first of a long line of Kings, or, if not of Kings, of Chief Magistrates, exercising with greater freedom and elasticity all the functions of Kings; but from the day that Charles the First was beheaded the restoration of Charles the Second became merely a question of time. However dignified by prudence, moderation, and sagacity, Cromwell's government was essentially a military despotism; and among a free people military despotisms are short-lived.

The solution of the constitutional problems which were involved in the contest between Charles and his Parliament was, by the shock to public feeling, delayed for a generation. The delay, however, was not perhaps to be regretted. The violent men on either side died out. The heroes of the Commonwealth, the fanatics whose spiritual pains and mental needs had torn England asunder, passed away. The passion of the Puritan would have been as prejudicial to a wise and prudent settlement as the passion of the Cavalier. Under an easy and somewhat cynical sovereign passion had time to cool. The mental balance was restored. And though the wave fell back, the tide did not turn. What might have been done in 1649 was done better in 1689. The conditions altogether were more favourable. The tropical had been exchanged for the temperate zone; the explosion had cleared the air.

The new race of reformers, indeed, were as different as men could be from the old; not better possibly, but better suited for the time. It is impossible to imagine a Halifax or a Somers sharing the spiritual exaltation, the mystical and visionary rapture, of a Lambert or a Vane. "Did'st thou stand forth by my worthy friend, and bear him company? Did thy soul suffer with him and rejoice with him, riding in his chariot of triumph to the block, to the axe, to the crown, to the banner, to the bed and ivory throne of the Lord God, thy Redeemer?" The constitutional Whig, steady, sagacious, moderate, never unselfishly imprudent, never finely intemperate,—is the creation of the last thirty or forty years of the Seventeenth Century.

Charles II., if the worst of Kings, was certainly the pleasantest of companions. Perfectly unaffected and perfectly fearless, he did not hesitate to mix with his subjects in the most familiar manner. And he had a shrewd eye both for men and books. He had acquired his experience, indeed, in a school which had aged him before his time. He was an old man at the Restoration. "I never till this day observed that the King was mighty gray," Pepys writes about 1662. In his careless brilliancies we see a mind of great natural parts that had been permitted to run to seed. Good-humoured, if somewhat cynical, toleration was his habitual mood. His courtiers might quiz him: he only laughed. When he heard of Rochester's famous epigram, he observed: "Quite true: my sayings are my own, my doings are those of my ministers." Shaftesbury, with his usual felicity, said that under King Charles the unfortunate fell lightly; and had Charles consulted his own feelings he would never have sent anything sharper than a jest or an epigram after his bitterest enemies. Of certain conspicuous but prudent conspirators of his reign he was content to observe with admirable neatness that they "committed treason by advice of counsel." But though habits of indulgence had weakened the spring of his mind, it still retained a fine edge. If it be true that Shirley's memorable lines were greatly admired by him, he must clearly have possessed a capacity for appreciating poetry of the highest class. Charles, it is true, starved his poets; but so long as they did not weary him with importunities, he was pleased to meet them and have them about him. He was frankly intimate with Waller and Dryden. He told the former, it is said, that his ode on Cromwell was superior to that on himself. "Poets, sire," was the witty apology, "succeed better in fiction than in truth." Not unfrequently, of a morning, the King might be seen with Dryden in St. James's Park, conversing familiarly about the last rhyming play or the new book of poems. Charles appears to have had a real regard for Dryden; he was always ready to defend him when assailed, telling those critics, for instance, who charged the laureate with theft, that he only wished they would steal him plays like Dryden's; and Dryden, on his side, who loved the great, was intoxicated by this flattering intimacy with Royalty.

The Revolution of 1689 was made inevitable by the stupid perversity and sour fanaticism of James. He invited disaster. By the exercise of ordinary tact and prudence the crisis might have been delayed for ten, or twenty, or thirty years. But James had neither tact nor prudence; and he rushed blindly upon his fate. The people did not love him; the nobles distrusted him; even the clergy, whose loyalty was proverbial, had been alienated and alarmed. He contrived with singular infelicity in less than four years to make himself impossible. The march of William of Orange from Torbay to London was a triumphal pageant; and when James fled from his palace he did not leave a friend behind him.

The hundred years which followed the revolution of 1689 were those during which England was ruled by what Mr. Disraeli was pleased to call the Venetian Oligarchy,—in other words the great Whig houses. It was not the Whig nobles only who ruled,—the Tories had their frugal share of power; but the general proposition that the House of Lords was relatively powerful for the whole of the eighteenth century can hardly be controverted. Thus the transfer of authority from one body in the State to another has been gradually effected. Only once in our Parliamentary history have we had to retrace our steps. King—Lords—Commons: from Elizabeth to Victoria there has been no such passionate or spasmodic action as violently to shake the springs of the Constitution except when Eliot and Pym and Cromwell held the reins. The powers that they sought to exercise have been *gradually* acquired by the Commons; and even to-day the prerogatives of the Sovereign and the privileges of the Church are wider all round than the Roundheads would have left them.

THE JUXON MEDAL

Throughout the Anglican Church for two hundred years a special prayer was offered on the day that Charles Stuart was executed. It besought Almighty God, "who in Thy heavy displeasure didst suffer the life of our Gracious Sovereign King Charles the First to be (as this day) taken away by the hands of cruel and bloody men," not to lay "the guilt of this innocent blood to the charge of the people of this land nor let it ever be required of us or our posterity." Charles may not have been a "martyr;" but those who brought him to the block were not wise: and the service, as a measure of their lack of wisdom, might have been suffered to remain. It was to say the least an interesting historical memorial: and the destruction of interesting historical memorials, which throw light upon the life of a nation, is not to be commended. And if Charles deserves to be remembered anywhere, it is by and within the Church, to which he adhered with constant and singular fidelity.

# CONTENTS.

## TEXT.



## LIST OF ILLUSTRATIONS.

THIS EDITION

# CHARLES I.,

BY

SIR JOHN SKELTON, K.C.B.,

HAS BEEN PRINTED AND THE PLATES HAVE BEEN ENGRAVED

BY JEAN BOUSSOD, MANZI, JOYANT & CO.,

At Asnières-sur-Seine,

near Paris.

[illegible]

# Charles I.

Sir JOHN SKELTON, K.C.B.

ILLUSTRATIONS

*From Contemporary Works of Art.*

# CHARLES I.

BY

SIR JOHN SKELTON, K.C.B.

GOUPIL & CO.,
FINE ART PUBLISHERS.
JEAN BOUSSOD, MANZI, JOYANT & CO.,
SUCCESSORS,
FINE ART PUBLISHERS TO HER MAJESTY.

LONDON: 25, BEDFORD STREET, STRAND. | PARIS: 24, BOULEVARD DES CAPUCINES.

EDINBURGH:
W. BROWN, 26, PRINCES STREET.

1898.

www.ingramcontent.com/pod-product-compliance
Lightning Source LLC
Chambersburg PA
CBHW020940030726
47496CB00005B/1276
* 9 7 8 3 7 4 2 8 6 4 9 6 3 *